Nobody Cares
Rydon Tyme: The Life of the Eye

Ali Muhammad

Nobody Cares is a fictitious story inspired by historic events, imaginative thoughts, and real life experiences of the writer.

Published by Leaders of Tomorrow, Today LLC
PO Box 470 Oshtemo, MI 49077
First Edition

ISBN-13: 978-0-578-52331-6
ISBN-10: 0-578-52331-0

Front and Back Cover Illustrator: Jamal Mayo
Editor: M. Araujo
Graphic Designer: LOTT Art Department
Story Illustrator: Aires Melo

Dedication

This book is dedicated to you, the reader. After teaching for 6 years, I've learned that every child has a story and children grow up to be adults. Life has a lot of cause and effect already in motion. Adults weren't born adults, we had to grow up first. Think about what you wanted to do most as a child, now make it happen if you haven't already.

I also dedicate this book to my family, friends, supporters, the Brother Cities: Detroit and Highland Park. All the people in West Michigan and around the world, thank you for all that you do.

Be sure to visit www.LOTT48203.com for books, blogs, careers, competitions, interviews, magazines, photo albums, press conferences, scholarship information, LOTT Sportswear, and more.

CONTENTS

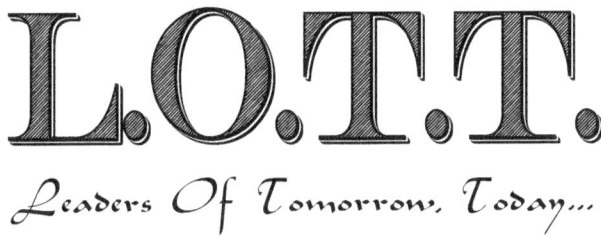

"MAKE A SPLASH IN THE WORLD"

WWW.LOTT48203.COM

10/23/2009

~~Dear Detective Tyme: Dr.~~
Dear Detective Dr. Rydon Tyme

My mama always tells me, if someone goes to school long enough to become a Dr., you better respect them enough to call them by their name. Sorry my letter is so sloppy, but this is my last piece of paper. Mama told me to bring my writing notebook home or ask Mr. Bright for a new notebook. I don't think he'll say no, but that notebook belongs to the next person who fills up their pages with math and journal writing stuff. ~~What~~ If everyone asked Mr. Bright for a notebook to take home then no one would have a notebook at all. Our school needs a lot of help. I don't want to make this sound like a pity party invitation... but it really is.

I don't think anybody can help us except you Sir. I've read your books, watched your shows over and over since I was a little girl. I'm eleven now. The second oldest of five kids my mom had. My big brother, Kimani, and I have the same daddy. My little sister Aliya and the twins, Traci and Terry have a different daddy.

We've seen every episode of Rydon Tyme's Unsolved Mysteries. The way you solved crimes people gave up on always got us excited. We play Tyme's Heroes at home all the time. My big brother knows how to act just like you. He can do your laugh and everything. Sometimes he fools the twins by acting like you and they think you're here. I wish my brother did more things like that at school. He would be really good in the plays but he's always in trouble.

Mom keeps telling him he's going to end up in jail like our daddy, if he doesn't turn it around. If I didn't know any better, I'd think he wanted to be in there with daddy the way he acts sometimes. My mom says he's just being a teenager, but just because he's thirteen doesn't mean he don't know how to act no more.

Enough about him, I'm your biggest fan, Dr. Tyme. I don't know how I know, but I <u>KNOW</u> you can help us if you ever get a chance to read my letters. I bet you probably get a lot of mail. That's why I started writing you every year on the same date since I was seven, hoping one day I'll get lucky. I'm going to start drawing on my envelopes. That will make them stand out more. I don't know if you'll ever get to read this letter, but we could really use your help, Mister Sir.

Love,

Nia Henrik
5th grade Honor Roll student at Elmwood Academy

```
Highland Park, Michigan
Elmwood Academy
2:21pm Eastern Standard Time
2009 October 23, Friday
```

"I need all eyes on me. Today we will be preparing for our chapter four test. Chapter four discusses the American Revolution and its effect on other nations around the world. Who can talk about a few events leading up to the American Revolution? Travis what do you think?"

"I think the Boston Tea Party was the coolest thing ever. They took the law in their own hands. If you have to go out, you might as well go out swinging."

"How many of you all agree with Mr. Moss?"

"More than I expected," Mr. Bright thought aloud to himself. "Let's break down what Mr. Moss just said. I'll write his three points in different colors, so we can easily distinguish the difference. Our topic is what Mr. Moss?"

"The Boston Tea Party," Travis answered.

"Good. First, Mr. Moss said the Boston Tea party was the coolest thing ever. Then he mentioned liking that they took the law into their own hands. And if you have to go out, go out with a fight. Excuse me. You said, 'you might as well go out swinging.' Did I get everything?"

"Yes," Travis smirked, confidently backing his point of view.

"Why was it so cool? Anybody," Mr. Bright paused. "Rachel?" he pointed to the back of the classroom.

"I thought it was cool because they fought for what was right," she answered with a shrug.

"What do you mean by *right*?" Mr. Bright replied with squinted eyebrows.

Rachel's pen tapped on her desk at a metronome's pace while she pondered her response. "You know, like the right thing to do," she answered, summing up her thoughts.

"What does the *right thing* mean?" Mr. Bright countered to the class.

"I'm asking you all this because the British called these *cool* people who took the law into their hands *rebels*. Then there were the *patriots*.

I'll let you find out who they were on your own while you read. You all have twenty minutes to work by yourselves or with a partner. You are to define either rebel or patriot. Whichever side your group is assigned, sway me your way based on your point of view."

Chatter scattered around the classroom like a stadium wave. Everyone was excited for the next great debate. Mr. Bright was a teacher by day and an Editor at night for the Highland Park Sun newspaper.

Every Friday, his students were given a topic to debate. Each team's job was to sway Mr. Bright their way. The winning writer had their work published in the upcoming Sunday newspaper.

"Teams four and one are to agree with Great Britain who called the frustrated colonists, *rebels*. Teams three and two, you are the *rebels* who want us to believe otherwise.

"As usual, you all have ten minutes to write, another ten minutes to share with a partner before we come together as a class. Are there any questions?" The silence surrounding them gave Mr. Bright confirmation to continue.

"While you are writing, keep Mr. Moss' statements in mind. They are still on the board written in red, black, and green. You may begin. Remember, writers work in silence," Mr. Bright reminded his pupils as he started the timer stationed at the front of the class.

While his students worked toward their deadlines, so did he. During his fifteen-year career, Mr. Bright mastered the third eye technique, a skill he learned from a mentor in the 1990s. He'd see a student wasting time, turn around and correct their behavior by looking in the opposite direction.

Once his students believed their teacher had three eyes, behavior problems drastically reduced. Some of the Highland Park Sun's best publications were put in motion during his class' independent writing assignments.

Isaac Bright was a thirty-six-year-old dreamer who never woke up. As he aged, his dreams became goals and his goals became accomplishments. A weekly newsletter to communicate with the families of his students led to establishing, *Bright Light,* a section in the newspaper used to showcase schools in the district. Thousands of subscribers counted on Mr. Bright's reports every Sunday for their early morning read over breakfast.

Ding ding ding!

With his palm resting on the silver bell at the far left podium closest to his desk, Mr. Bright set the tone for opening arguments as he reset the timer. "Team four and one who will be speaking for the group?"

"Angel," they answered.

"Team three and two, same question?"

"Nia," the teams agreed.

"Angelica Sorrento and Nia Henrik please take you places at the podiums provided for you at the front of the class. Give them some help everyone, two claps and a snap."

CLAP! CLAP! SNAP! The class responded.

"Would either of you like to go first?"

"I'll go first," Angelica responded quickly, flipping her hair habitually.

"Very well, please give Miss Sorrento your undivided attention while she defends Great Britain for labeling certain colonists, *rebels.*"

A rebel is a person who opposes an established ruler or government.

Even though the Rebels thought what they were doing was right, rules are around for a reason. My mom makes me straighten my bed every morning. I don't know why. I'm going to mess it up again later, but I do it anyway. She tells us every Saturday that chores are our way of paying rent. She said until we get jobs to help pay the bills or get our own place, we have to do our chores. If we didn't do what she asked, my mom would probably call us rebels too. We have to do these things now while we're kids so that we'll know what to do when we grow up.

My mom is kind of like Great Britain and the rebels are like kids who are in a hurry to grow up like my uncle always says. Great Britain sent the Colonists to the Americas to be the rulers of the New World. If they would have listened to Great Britain the way we listen to our parents, the country might be better than it is now."

"I like how you compared Great Britain and the Colonist to you and your mother. It gave us something to relate to. Great job. Next, we need all eyes and ears on Miss Henrik. She will be defending the *rebels* who considered themselves *patriots*."

Patriots are people who love their country strong enough to defend it against injustice.

I'm a patriot but people call me a rebel, and I will never understand why. I fight for what's right and no other reason. In the beginning of the year, Mr. Bright gave us all a copy of the United States' Bill of Rights. Our history books have the rest of the constitution in the back after the glossary.

Until last month, I didn't know our country had rules and laws because no one acts like it. Think about what we see on the news now compared to tea and taxes being news back then.

People called Patrick Henry and Ben Franklin patriots in those days because they stood up for what they believed in. Even though some still called them rebels.

I guess what I'm trying to say is, I can relate to rebels sometimes because most of us are just misunderstood. Anytime I get in trouble, it's for taking up for other people and if that makes me a rebel, oh well. But according to American history, I'm the most patriotic.

The class erupted like the a volcano in a science fair project.

"Nia! Nia! Nia!"

"Very passionate speech, Miss Henrik. I love how you tied history into your argument. Your Benjamin Franklin and Patrick Henry comparison really put things into perspective. Someone's actions done in good faith, can seem otherwise.

Alright class, you know the drill. When it's a close call like this, I need your help. Cast your vote for today's winner and two reasons why. I will tally up the results before the end of the day.

Stack your writing notebooks on your tables, opened to today's debate. You all have forty-five minutes to finish reading chapter four and answer the critical thinking questions that follow. Are there any questions?

The clock is ticking. Get busy," Mr. Bright concluded, snapping his fingers as the class clapped twice instinctively.

Elmwood Academy differed from the other middle schools in the district. It was referral based. Only students recognized as gifted and talented, or extremely hardworking were recommended for Elmwood Academy.

Large class sizes weren't an issue because students came to school anxious for knowledge.

As with any school, bonds were formed, merged, and broken with regularity. They brought in students from all over the city and as they grew older, they matured. As did their egos and personalities.

"I'm not voting for Nia. Are you? She always wins," Cassandra asked her elbow partner.

"It's because Mr. Bright feels bad for her since she's always in trouble. He has to make her feel good about herself, he's a teacher. It's his job," Desiree responded, casting her vote.

"Don't be a hater your whole life, Desi," Samantha said, taking a break from her work. "Nia is bad sometimes but she's the smartest kid in the school."

"She's not smarter than me. Besides, if she's so smart why is she always in trouble then? Answer me that!" Cassandra laughed, pointing with the eraser of her mechanical pencil.

"Because of people like you. Why do I hear my name from the other side of the room, little girl?" Nia asked taking a seat at the table.

"Little? I'm older than you," Cassandra reminded her.

"Whatever. The next time I hear you talking about me when I'm not around, you're going to regret it, *little* girl.

"I'm not scared of you, Nia" Cassandra said, cleaning her nails with the clip on her pencil.

"You don't have to be scared of me. Just know that if I have to come back, it's going to be a problem," Nia said, pushing her index finger against the side Cassandra's head, all while the class stared on, waiting for the bout of the week.

"Miss Henrik and Miss Anderson, I need to see you two in the hallway, now," Mr. Bright's voice sounded from the front of the classroom.

Mr. Bright kept things private. Any discussions regarding student misconduct wasn't a class issue. It was confidential. Only to be shared with administration, parents, guardians, and whatever unlucky student was involved. This allowed him to levy a fair punishment without the eyes and ears of the classroom casting judgment.

"Mr. B, she started it," Nia pointed.

"That's a lie I didn't do anything to you," Cassandra replied quickly with a broken face, complete with teary eyes.

"Enough. Nia, what happened?" Mr. Bright asked with a heavy bass in his voice.

"I was reading chapter four and got distracted because I kept hearing Cassandra and Desiree saying my name."

"Cassandra?" Mr. Bright motioned.

"I was talking about her, but it wasn't bad. All I said was that she's always in trouble and it's true. Look where we are now. I've never even been in the principal's office before," she bawled.

"Do you know what I heard from the both of you just now? It sounds like the two people who need to stay out of each other's business. You come to school to learn not to fight. Leave this nonsense out of my classroom. Am I clear?"

"Yes, Mr. Bright," Cassandra answered quickly.

"Yes, Mr. B," Nia replied.

"If you don't like each other, that's part of life. You're not always going to get along with everyone, but you will respect each other. If I have to talk to either of you again about this, I'm calling home and I'll see you after school for detention. Are either of you finished with the assignment?"

"No."

"Nope."

"So, do you really have time to waste?" Mr. Bright asked.

"No."

"No, Mr. B."

"Then please stop wasting my time and yours. Shake hands, have a seat, and finish your work," Mr. Bright said and motioned toward the door, welcoming the girls back into the classroom.

Highland Park, Michigan
Elmwood Academy
3:45pm Eastern Standard Time
2009 October 23, Friday

"Have a great weekend everyone. Be sure to work on your projects at home. They're due next month. Do not procrastinate or else it'll show. Class dismissed," Mr. Bright said holding up the peace sign with one hand, closing the daily read aloud with the other.

Filing out the door, students were eager to enjoy their two day getaway. They swarmed to the bus stop like bees on honey. Boys wore Junior League Football jerseys representing different teams around the Brother Cities of Highland Park and Detroit.

Engaged in their weekly verbal disputes, the boys were getting ready to miss another occurrence that was equally as predictable. "I heard my name again. You're still running your mouth about me, really?" Nia said, confronting Cassandra by the bus stop.

"Leave me alone, Nia," Cassandra replied, looking over her shoulder, finishing her conversation.

"I will after I say what I need to say. If I hear my name in your mouth and you're not talking to me, it's going to be you and me, Sandra."

"Okay, I heard you in class. Get out of my face," Cassandra said, avoiding Nia by any means.

"Nia, no… Let's go! You know what mama said," Aliya pleaded, tugging her sister's hand.

"You better listen to your sister. You know what mama said," Cassandra giggled in a huddle with her friends.

Nia's razor sharp eyes lacerated Cassandra's flesh. Her facial expression read fear and her eyes told the same story. Satisfied with Cassandra's response, Nia took the highroad and walked off with her arm around her little sister.

"You're right, Liya. Come on. Did you have a good day in school today?" Nia inquired.

"Yup, I got an A on my spelling test!" Aliya smiled. A wide grin revealed a gap in her lower row of teeth.

"Liya! What happen to your tooth?"

"Nothing. It's right here," Aliya assured her, as it rattled in a large plastic tooth container that she received from the main office. "It was stuck in my apple after I bit it," she pouted.

"You know what happens to baby teeth right?" Nia gloated.

"I don't know. I tried to put it back, but it wouldn't stay in," Aliya said playing with the empty space between her teeth.

"You're so funny, Liya. You can't put it back. These kinds of things happen while you grow up. Pretty soon you'll be a big girl like me with all your grownup teeth."

"Her baby sister is more mature than she is and she's in first grade. I love Aliya, that's my girl," Cassandra said pumping her fist, laughing with her friends from a distance.

Stopping in her tracks, rage filled Nia's body and the only color she could see was red.

"Wait here, Liya," she quietly ordered her sister.

"Nia, no!" Aliya squealed, waving her arms, with a crumbled look on her face.

Storming off with a head full of steam toward the group of girls, Nia picked out the familiar voice of the bunch and pushed its owner to the pavement.

"What did I just tell you!?" Nia shouted.

The group of girls quickly dispersed in search of help.

Towering over her, Nia blocked the sun with her body. "Get up!" she yelled.

Cassandra stood to her feet, fearful of Nia's next course of action. Witnessing Nia make an example out of many girls in her class, she anticipated being next. "I don't want to fight you, Nia," she stammered.

"I think you do," Nia answered promptly. "Stand up... Cassandra."

"Nia, let's go home pleassssse," Nia turned toward her sister. Looking into Aliya's impressionable little eyes, she knew it wasn't the time to fight.

"You're not even worth getting suspended over," Nia sighed, hanging her head. "Next time, I'll be over you like an eclipse," Nia warned, pointing her finger at Cassandra. A ripple of laughter erupted from the group of boys gathered by the flag poles.

"Like an eclipse though?" one boy laughed, falling dramatically to the ground.

"You can tell she smart," another joked.

Intimidated by her foe, Cassandra attacked hoping to swing the momentum in her favor and with all her might, she pushed.

Tripping over her little sister, Aliya broke Nia's fall. Her tear ducts opened, flooding her dark brown eyes. Both knees were skinned to white flesh, leaking blood onto the cement.

Half the crowd disbursed for help. The boys suppressed their jokes to carry Aliya inside. Nia balled her fist and released two punches that landed on Cassandra's jawbone and forehead.

Dang!

The crowd responded as Cassandra returned to the pavement she'd just departed. Using her hands to shield the punches, Cassandra covered her head, hoping to reduce the damage inflicted upon her.

Nia continued pounding Cassandra's body and any other openings she saw available. Seconds before landing a stomp to the midsection, Mr. Bright rushed to the scene with the group of girls who sought after him.

Picking Nia up into the air, he was able to restrain her before she touched down. "Go to the office, Nia!" Mr. Bright said with a raised voice and pointed to the door.

"But, Mr. B?"

"TO THE OFFICE!" he yelled.

Nia's eyes filled with tears as she ran across the field and down the hall to the school's main office.

"Cassandra, are you okay? Let's go inside so we can call home."

Helping Cassandra to her feet, Mr. Bright escorted his battered and bruised student to the principal. Grabbing his attention, the minute he walked in the room, were Nia's bloodshot red eyes.

He had never seen Nia shed tears. In the past, she always took accountability for her actions, accepted the consequences and moved on with her day. The way she looked at Mr. Bright made him feel like he failed her.

Locking eyes with his most outspoken student once again, she instantly looked away in the opposite direction. After delivering another crack to her heart, Nia slumped into her seat, tuning out the man who was once one of her favorite people.

Coming into the world a blank canvas, her innocence was slowly chipped away with each passing day of her life. Everyone she ever trusted betrayed her some way or another.

"Did you see what happen, Bright?" a voiced rung from the back office.

"No sir, just the end. These two have been going back and forth with each other all day. It started in Social Studies. I thought they quashed it, but I guess I was wrong," Mr. Bright said, shaking his head.

"We did quash it," Nia announced.

"If that's quashing it, I must blind. You were getting ready to *squash* this young lady's ribcage before I stepped in," Mr. Bright reminded her.

"You weren't even there Mr. Bright. You don't know what happened," she shot back.

The bite of honesty stunned him like a bee sting. Mr. Bright had been redirecting Nia since the first grade. Not necessarily because of her behavior. She would get lost wandering down the first floor hallway before being steered in the right direction.

Every year on the last day of school, Nia made it a point to find Mr. Bright during the school's Field Day activity sponsored by the Parent Support Club to say, 'I can't wait until I'm in your class Mr. B.' He was never *Mr. Bright.*

She admired him as a teacher because of his consistency. He ran a tight ship and Nia never had a teacher who listened to her side of the story before casting judgment. That reason alone made her anxious to be in a class where justice was served for *all.*

Dr. Holcomb leaned back in his seat, choosing his next words wisely. "You were there Nia, what happen?"

Dr. Grant Holcomb was a jack of all trades. A retired Chief of Police turned psychologist. His job as Principal in one of Michigan's most successful schools became his third career.

"It didn't start in Social Studies. It started on the bus this morning. Cassandra and her friends kept picking on Charlotte. I know I said I'd let the adults handle it, but you know how it is on the bus. Charlotte was crying so I sat next to her."

Both men sat motionless hearing the day's events unfold before their eyes.

"Then she threw away my lunch while I was still eating. I was two seconds from hitting her then, but the lunch lady saw it all and gave me another plate."

"It was time to go," Cassandra sassed.

"Cassandra please. Continue Nia," Dr. Holcomb said, wrinkling his face with disgust.

"Thank you. Like I was saying before I was rudely interrupted," Nia said rolling her eyes away from Cassandra. "I was about to hit her then, but the lunch lady saved her. Dr. Holcomb I'm really trying to stay out of trouble, but she's been getting on my nerves all day and I *know* she's doing it on purpose."

"You *think* she's doing it on purpose. Unless you heard it from her, it's not a fact. Facts only please. If too many rumors spread through the winds, we'll all end up with at least one by mistake. Finish the story," Dr. Holcomb requested, spinning his plush leather chair on wheels toward the window.

"After we rotated for Social Studies, we got into it and Mr. Bright took us in the hallway. I thought we quashed it all, but she started talking about me again after school to her little flunkies. Right in front of my face! Trying me."

"Enough with the names, Nia Henrik. We get the point. Finish," Dr. Holcomb said, waving his hand.

"I apologize. I was going to fight her sooner, but my sister talked me out of it. Sandra---"

"Ca-ssandra," she corrected. "We aren't friends anymore."

"Sandra…" Nia repeated, "said she didn't want to fight and the next thing I know, she pushed me when I was turning around and made me fall on my baby sister. Her arm and legs were bloody, and I couldn't take it anymore, she deserved it."

"Cassandra is this true?" Dr. Holcomb asked aloud and with facial disgust.

"Yes, but she came over to me. I was scared, Dr. Holcomb. I didn't know what else to do. I thought if I didn't get her first, she would get me. I did *not* mean to hurt your sister, Nia. I am so sorry."

"You are sorry," Nia replied.

"Miss Henrik!" Dr. Holcomb barked, having enough with the disrespect.

"I mean… I accept your apology," Nia answered.

"What do you think, Mr. Bright? I'll leave it up to you."

"After school detention for Miss Henrik until Cassandra's suspension is over…"

"Suspension?" Cassandra questioned with a cracking voice.

"I wish it didn't have to come to this Cassandra. I really do. Nia, call your Mother and let her know she needs to pick you up at 5:30 p.m." Knowing Nia's situation at home, Mr. Bright knew an at-home suspension wouldn't be the most beneficial.

"Cassandra, I'm disappointed. I expect more from you. I didn't know you could be so sneaky and that saddens me. I want you to think about your actions and come back to school Wednesday, ready to work."

"Detention, effectively immediately for Miss Henrik and a two-day suspension for Miss Anderson, it has been written," Dr. Holcomb documented before removing his reading glasses.

Walking the corridors of the building, squeaking gym shoes and the clacking sound of Mr. Bright's big, block, dress shoes echoed down the hallway. Having reached their destination, the motion censored lights activated, illuminating the room at their arrival.

"Have a seat, Nia."

Still angry at the world, Nia took a seat without saying a word. "Nia, I should have listened to you before yelling at you the way I did. I was wrong and for that, I apologize."

"I accept your apology, Mr. Bright."

Taking a seat at his desk, Mr. Bright logged into his computer in search of Nia's contact information. "I know you're upset with me Nia but that won't change anything. You were about to finish that young lady off and things could have gotten really bad from there.

There could have been criminal charges filed and it wouldn't have mattered who was right or wrong. Both of your parents would have spent hundreds, if not thousands, on court costs and lawyer fees," Mr. Bright informed Nia from an adult's perspective.

"I don't care," she replied.

"I know you don't, but I do, and I care about your future. Probably more than you do at this stage in your life.

You're way too smart to throw your life away Nia. One mistake can change your whole life and when I saw how angry you looked before you went to kick her. It took me back to my childhood days."

Nia's head tilted a slight right. She always thought teachers were perfect people, never considering they had lives before standing in front of a classroom. Especially Mr. Bright.

"One of my best friends from school reminds me of you. He was one of the smartest students in the school, if not the smartest. When we were in elementary school, he was one of the nicest kids in the city. By the time we got to middle school the world changed him. What do you think I mean by that?"

17

"People probably took his kindness for weakness," Nia answered.

"In a nutshell, yes, that's exactly what I meant. He was always giving people his lunch, pencils, stickers, nickels to buy candy after school. You name it, he gave it. After a while, people started taking his things without asking and by the end of the year, he was getting picked on by every bully in fifth grade.

"I was like you. I hated seeing people who couldn't defend themselves get picked on, but I was wrong about him. He beat up a kid twice his size one day in the locker room and it created a monster.

He didn't care about school anymore and his behavior carried over into the summer. By the time we started sixth grade, his heart had already turned cold. He'd get in fights at least once or twice a month. Do you know where he is now?"

"In jail?"

"Worse," Mr. Bright dismissed.

"Gone?"

"Even worse than that," he rejected.

Nia was confused. Those were the only two things she had been warned of if her attitude didn't change. She heard it so much, it no longer had an effect. It became trivial, more so than an effective scared straight tactic.

"What could be worse than those two?"

"He's a thirtysomething-year-old fifth grader."

Nia cracked a smile for the first time in over a day.

"It's not funny, I'm serious. He can't read too good, write, divide, or multiply because he hasn't practiced any of it since we were your age and sometimes, if you don't use it, you lose it.

He can always get it back but why mess it up in the first place? I saw him not too long ago and he looks old enough to be my father. Life is hard without knowledge, Nia. It's hard enough with it."

A pair of feet with quick strides could be heard long before it's arrival. "Sounds like your mother?" Mr. Bright assumed.

"Girl, what did I tell you about getting in trouble just last Friday?" Ms. Henrik said entering the classroom in a blue polo shirt and black work pants. "Hi, Mr. Bright. I apologize for keeping you here so late on the weekend, again," Nancy pleaded, giving Nia a withering look she tried her best to avoid.

Isaac Bright and Nancy Henrik had been allies for a long time. A few years prior, Mr. Bright taught her eldest son. A bruiser like Nia who lacked self-control. Although he respected great leadership, he equally resented those who failed to get the job done.

During his time with Mr. Bright, Kimani Henrik earned a flawless 4.0 grade point average and was voted *Student of the Year* by the teachers, staff, and students. His essays won contests all over the world.

He was equally as productive in math, earning back-to-back Math Bowl Championship Cups. Students from around the world in his graduating class competed during Spring Break in Port Au Prince, Haiti.

The following spring, he successfully defended his title in Cairo, Egypt.

Kimani's accolades brought in flocks of literature from premier high schools around the country. After falling victim to the liberties of middle school the following year, his grades took a drastic dip and he was suspended regularly.

His offers no longer needed to be signed, sealed, or delivered. They had become null and void. "It's alright, Nancy. I was just telling Nia about Ramon Peters and how he was one of the smartest students in the city. Do you remember him?"

"He might have been all-world. I remember they would fly him to all those different places to read his essays. He always showed off his medals and trophies at lunch time as soon as he came back to school. Wow time flies. I remember that like it was yesterday. Nia knows him too."

"I do?" Nia replied with confusion.

"Ramon is the man who always asks to pump my gas. The one you and your brother say I always help."

"What happened to him?" Nia asked, full of curiosity.

"He couldn't stay out of trouble and it caught up to him after a while. People will work with children but once you grow up, nobody cares why you cut up. They just lock you up. One mistake can ruin your whole life," Nancy concluded.

"Does that sound familiar, Nia? I just told her the same thing. One mistake is all it takes. That's why I yelled at you; I saw *your* life flash before *my* eyes."

"You made Mr. Bright yell? I've known this man since we were younger than you and *I've* never heard him yell. We are going to have a long talk about this when we get home.

"You're going to write an apology letter too. Then read it to Mr. Bright and your classmates Monday morning. Go wait for me in the hallway," Nancy motioned.

"Mr. Bright can she have a sheet of paper?"

"Absolutely, take the stack on the counter with you on your way out, Nia," Mr. Bright said waving his hand.

Of all the lectures Nia received on her behavior, the tale of Ramon Peters hit her the hardest. Every day since she started walking to school, she noticed a man leaning against the wall in the alley of her apartment building. Not a day passed without her wondering his story and how he got in the condition he was in.

"Remember the little first grader that used to bite my ankles at Field Day to tell me how much she couldn't wait to be in my class?" Mr. Bright asked.

Nodding her head, Nia silently answered.

"Bring her with you to class on Monday. I miss that kid."

Laughing as she exited the room Nia extended a verbal peace treaty to her mentor. "Okay. See you Monday, Mr. B."

Nancy and Mr. Bright conversed in private to figure out a solution to the problem they were facing. "Thank you so much for not suspending her, Isaac. I know she can be a handful sometimes."

"No problem, Nancy. She's come a long way, I must say. I rarely have a problem with her in my class but the minute she's out of my sight, that's when issues occur.

"Lately she hasn't been the initiator. But she reacts, and the other students know it. I think they bother her just to get a response. That's the opposite of what was going on with her brother. They respected him so much they just wanted to be around him. So, they'd do whatever he did."

"I don't know why girls are so catty," Nancy said fiercely.

"You were the same way back in our day," Mr. Bright laughed.

"Here you go bringing up old stuff again," Nancy giggled, slapping his shoulder.

Hearing it all from the hall, Nia peeked in for a closer look. "In my defense, I wasn't a trouble-maker, thank you very much, sir. I was a finisher. Trouble vanished once it got to me, honey," Nancy joked.

"Now you sound like your daughter."

"Uh oh…"

The laughter filling the room, planted a smile on Nia's face as she drifted off to a happier place.

"How's Kimani doing? He's in high school now, right?"

"Almost, he's got one more year, and I promise I'm not sending him to Highland Park City High."

"Why is that?"

21

"He needs a fresh start. Do you think the High School for Higher Learning will take him, even though his grades aren't what they used to be?"

"That depends, has he been suspended?"

"That boy has been suspended more times than Zeek the Sleek."

"Wow, uhmm… well typically they don't accept students who have been suspended more than twice in a five year span. There are special cases such as passing the entrance exam with a 143 or higher with a letter of recommendation from their current principal. Or by lottery, that's when candidates are chosen by Educators who graduated from the school."

"You went there, didn't you?"

"Yes ma'am."

"Isaac, could you do me a favor?"

"You know I'd do anything for you Nancy. We go way back," Mr. Bright laughed, knowing what was coming his way. "But before I say yes, Kimani needs to talk to the boys in my class. They need to hear what I'm saying about leadership from someone closer to their age. Instead of just me all the time."

"Done. He won't like having to be away from his friends before high school, but he'll get over it," Nancy snickered with tough love. "I know what's best for him. I just don't want him to blow it like I did."

"You didn't blow it, Nancy," Mr. Bright rejected.

"What do you call it? I dropped out of college, fifteen credits short of graduation. Who does that? I'll go back when Kimani turns *two, three, four… ten*. Now it's really too late. I could've had my own PR firm by now."

"It's never too late Nancy," Mr. Bright reminded her, encouraging an old friend.

"Believe me, I've tried. I owe student loan debt. I have kids, Isaac. They all got taller and need new coats. This is Michigan, it could snow next week. That's my student loan payment right there," she said dismissing the pipe dream. "I blew it… Have a good weekend," Nancy waved, tired from a long day.

"Girl, why can't you ever stay out of trouble?" she scolded, as the two walked down the hallway.

"But mom," Nia pleaded.

"Enough with the 'but moms', Nia. You saw your sister's knees. I don't think it's enough Neosporin in the world to heal her skin without scarring. For you to be so smart, you sure do a lot things that don't make sense."

"Mom, I'm sorry."

"*You apologize*, you're *NOT* sorry. That's why I get so frustrated with you," Nancy said, storming out the building towards the school parking lot. Nia trailed behind with the school nurse, who wheeled out her sleeping sister.

Closing the door to a 2000 Pentagon Sledge Hammer, Nancy finished her speech, seamlessly holding back tears. "Nia, you don't understand how hard life is. You're too young. I was just talking to your teacher about my life and how I blew it because I never maximized my potential."

Nia's head hung in shame with the guilt of Aliya's injury weighing heavy on her heart. Looking to the back seat, Aliya was sleeping peacefully with heavily wrapped legs. "I apologize mom, I really do. I knew it wasn't worth it."

"Then why'd you do it? What if they never got Mr. Bright? We'd be in a police station instead of the principal's office, Nia," Nancy lectured.

"I gave up my dreams when I had your brother. My life has been on hold ever since. As soon as you're old enough to babysit, you're going to start helping out around the house. I'm picking up my dreams really soon sweetie. If you don't want to make the best of yourself, then I will.

```
          Highland Park, Michigan
               W Grand Street
     12:28am Eastern Standard Time
     2011 October 23, Sunday
```

10/23/2011

Dear Detective Dr. Rydon Tyme,

Last year, I drew a picture of you on the envelope, so I know you had to have seen it. But who knows? I think I'm finally accepting the fact that you left us. Everybody talks about how you haven't been seen since 1968 but you still release projects every few years. I don't know what to believe anymore.

The real reason I don't think you're with us is because on your shows and in your books, all you talk about is how you can't give up or take breaks. For you to not be here when we really need you, must mean that you're in a better place.

This year has been harder than I thought. Some of my best friends from elementary school act like we never met since we all got to middle school.

Elmwood is set up kind of weird but cool at the same time. It's called Elmwood Academy, but it's 2 schools on the same campus. One building is for the elementary school, grades 1-6. The other building, where I go now is the middle school, grades 7-8.

I guess it makes sense why they stay away from me now. I've been in fights with girls from a lot of different circles in the school. If they hang out with me, they'll have to go through what I go through every other day.

Being forced to be a loner has taught me a lot about myself, Dr. Tyme. People can't make me mad the way they used to in elementary school.

Like my pictures? I started drawing again. It puts me in a peaceful place. Sometimes I pretend to be in the places I draw. I drew a picture of our family sitting on thrones in Ancient Egypt for one of my brother's class projects last year. He liked it so much he had it framed and made into t-shirts that he wears under his game jerseys.

I put a lot of work into my art, hours. All day and night sometimes. I love the feeling of finishing a project. I just got done with a couple of paintings before writing this letter. I skip sleep to draw like you used to skip sleep for law.

If you thought last year's picture was nice, wait until you see this year's. It's going to be of me and you. It will be so great you'll have to come back and change the world once and for all.

Your best friend,
Nia Henrik

P.S. I haven't been suspended all year!

P.S.S. We miss you, Dr. Tyme!

Highland Park, Michigan
W Grand Street
5:55am Eastern Standard Time
2011 October 23, Sunday

With all that she had been through in thirteen years of life, Nia learned to sleep rather lightly. At 6 a.m. she could hear her mother packing luggage, paired with the scent of curling irons and freshly brewed green tea. The smell of honey vapors and maple syrup, snuck in through the keyhole of Nia's bedroom door, waking her from her sleep.

Gazing at her personal bathroom of their historic Michigan home, Nia contemplated making the trip. Her other option was to lay peacefully while the familiar sound of her spare key was put to use.

Just as she suspected, her mother entered the room with a delicious proposition.

"Nia, baby. Wake up," Nancy said, shaking the body of one only pretending to be asleep. "Ni...a. Nia, Nia, mommy's here to see you," she repeated with a cadence.

Rolling to her stomach to hide her smile, Nia smelled pancakes, corn grits, beef sausage, and eggs of course. Although overloaded with suspense on whether the eggs were scrambled or an omelet, Nia wouldn't fold easily.

"I see you smiling, wake up Nia Pia. I made you breakfast," Nancy said rubbing her daughter's back.

"Mom, it is too early," she replied, ducking her head under the covers. Hiding from the 40-watt light bulb, glowing from the globe shaped lamp atop her desk.

"If you don't eat it, Liya or the twins will, and you can have their oatmeal," Nancy smiled.

"Leave it. I'll get to it after it cools... and the sun rises," she mumbled.

"If you insist, but the cheese in that omelet won't stay stringy for long," Nancy added, sipping tea from her mug.

Snatching the covers from her face, Nia tossed her pillow next to her laptop on the loveseat. "I knew you liked my omelets but geez. Honey, I'm flattered," Nancy blushed. "While you're in such a good mood, I need you to watch the kids, me and the girls are taking a trip," Nancy said on her way out the door.

You know these are YOUR children, right? Nia thought to herself, as she took a bite from her morning feast. "All day?" she wondered.

"Today and tomorrow night. Your granny will be by in the morning. I went grocery shopping yesterday and left some money under the fruit bowl. Only call if you need to. I'll text you when we get there and when I'm headed back."

"You know what Traci said to me yesterday?" Nia responded completely off topic.

"What?" Nancy answered quickly, anxious for an update.

"Mommy… she called me mommy," Nia replied, cutting her omelet.

"Traci is something else, she's young. She's still learning where she is," Nancy paused, before sipping her tea.

"The twins are almost three now mom," Nia reasoned.

"Nia, spare me. You sound like your grandmother. The twins know who I am and what they mean to me. Just like you, Aliya, and your brother."

"I apologize, mom," Nia said with a bowed head, taking another bite from her breakfast. *I tried.*

A long nap after an early meal put Nia back in good spirits. After placing packages of instant oatmeal back into the cupboard, she removed a bowl from the kitchen cabinet.

Reaching for a fork from the drawer below the buffed marbled countertop, Nia turned on the stove's pilot light. Ready to give her sisters and baby brother the same early morning surprise as she. The scent of burning butter against the stainless steel pan set, signaled the last piece to the breakfast puzzle.

As she flipped an omelet into the air for personal practice, the door opened with applauses as the twins clapped in unison at the end of the show. "Do it again, mommy!" Traci yelled in admiration, running to hug Nia with a smile that touched Los Angeles and New York with the corners of her mouth.

"I'm your sister, Traci. We have the same mommy," Nia said sternly, hoping to get her point across.

"Where is she?" Traci wondered.

"Mommy just left. She'll be back in a couple days," Nia assured her.

"My sistah?" Traci asked with confusion.

Hanging her head, Nia's previous suspicions had been confirmed. Somehow, she and her mother traded places in her baby sister's eyes. Having filled in during her mother's reoccurring string of absences over the last few months, Nia was finally able to understand why.

"We're all going to laugh about this one day," Nia hugged back.

With breakfast over and done with, it was time for some recreational activities. A day at the park was a typical Sunday afternoon event for the Henrik family. It was a second home for Kimani and Nia when they were younger.

"Mommy, push me!" Traci shouted, waddling toward the swings. Pulling baby Terry with her.

"Mommy?" Kimani repeated, hearing it all from the basketball courts across the walkway. Kimani spent most his early mornings at the courtyard. He was either exercising, working on his jump shot, or practicing ball handling techniques.

"She won't stop calling me mommy, Ki," Nia complained.

Having analyzed the situation, Kimani quickly found the perfect solution, laughter. "It's not funny, Ki," Nia said playfully punching her older brother. "What if she grows up thinking I'm really her mom?" She continued.

"Then I guess you'd be Sister-Mom," Kimani joked from a hero pose six feet, four inches above ground level. "Mommy-Sister" he laughed again.

"I hope she knows who I am," Kimani quickly thought aloud.

"Come here Ci Ci," standing upright, no longer swinging on her stomach, little Traci ran toward the name used only by one person.

Please call him daddy that way it won't be just me, Nia thought over and over, watching the reunion closely.

"What's my name?" Kimani asked his baby sister.

"Kimani," little Traci answered, being airlifted to Kimani's broad shoulders.

"Where's mommy?" he wondered.

Traci looked to Nia and pointed with her left index finger. Seeing his baby sister refer to her own sister as mommy a second time, ignited another laughing spell from the eldest child. "Ci Ci, Nia is our sister, not our mommy," Kimani reasoned.

"Umm mmmm," she rejected, sliding down Kimani's body like a firehouse pole. Racing off once again for the U-shaped, rubber bottomed swing.

"How long has she been calling you that?" Kimani asked in a serious tone.

"It was her first word. I didn't think anything of it back then because she was calling everybody mommy. Then all of a sudden it was just me. Maybe if you were home sometimes, you'd know, Mr. PBL."

"We'll see what you say after you start getting letters in the mail with season tickets to watch me play in the Professional Basketball League. Real hoopers say the league's whole name. The same way MJ always says, *The game of basketball* instead of just *basketball*, make sense?"

"Here we go again," Nia snickered.

29

"Or when I invite you to the palace. I'm going to have it built for us in Egypt."

"Egypt?" she asked in wonderment.

"Yea, Egypt. Since I don't know where our roots are, I assume we come from Egyptian royalty," Kimani chuckled, releasing the ball from the gaps of his widely spread fingers, shooting a jump shot that snapped the nets.

Swish

"Well, I guess I better be quiet. I wouldn't want to mess that up," Nia laughed as she walked away to the sound of another successful flick of the wrist.

Swish

"Nothing but net, mommy!" he laughed still posing in poster form.

```
       Highland Park, Michigan
     Sandy's Burgers and Breakfast
     7:11pm Eastern Standard Time
        2011 October 23, Sunday
```

"Then I'm going to be a movie star. After that, I'll run for Senate, then President on my thirty-fifth birthday. When I'm done being president, I'm going to be a model like Gabby Powers. Then I'll direct movies, design clothes..."

Aliya went on and on about her future endeavors while the family waited for dinner turned breakfast. All Nia could do was reminisce on the days when she went through the same routine with their mother. She gave up on joining the police force and fire department at the same time. Lawyer turned Judge no longer appealed to her either.

After giving up on her dream jobs before having a hiring date, Nia took a full-time interest in the Arts when she was a few years older than Aliya. Something that started as anger management, turned into a hobby that revealed her purpose in life.

Letting her sister dream on, Nia patiently waited for a gap in the conversation, "Out of all those things you named, which would you do for free?" she asked hoping her sister would think hard about the question before giving an answer.

"All of them," Aliya shrugged.

"Pick one thing and focus on it, Liya. You can't do everything at the same time," Nia advised, searching the menu for something new.

"You pick one thing; I'm doing everything I want to do," Aliya smirked.

"That's why I love you, Aliya. You're so confident," Nia smiled, tickling her favorite girl.

Nia, Aliya, and the twins were busy coloring in white spots on their placemats when the food finally arrived. "One steak and egg combo with hash browns and an orange juice," the server said sitting Nia's plate in front of her. "And two, eggs, grits, and turkey sausage kid's meals with ice cold spring waters."

"I love bweakfast food," little Terry said kicking his feet from the high-chair. His chubby cheeks sprayed food all over the bib, shielding his amazingly clean white tee shirt.

"Thanks Nia," Terry said, chomping on a piece turkey sausage.

"Thank you," Traci added stuffing eggs where they belonged. Neither of the twins wasted time using a fork. Their hands were much more efficient.

With bloated bellies and carryout boxes in hand, Nia left a tip on the table and headed west on their way to Grand Street. Finally reaching their street corner, the foursome walked to their residence, holding hands with Nia on the outside.

Traci's familiarity for the neighborhood took over once she saw the family house. Shooting off in a sprint to cross the street, a black 1996 Pentagon Resurrection driving by marked the end. Baby Traci stared directly at the grill of a car in motion.

Racing to the curb behind her, Nia grabbed the back of Traci's jacket and yanked her to the grass. Honking his horn in fury, the man yelled, "Stay out of the street!" as he turned right on Woodward Avenue.

Neighbors watched on as Nia hugged little Traci harder than ever before, crying tears by the ounce. "What did I tell you about slipping away from me and running out in the street," she shouted, popping her bottom.

Tears from a broken heart flowed with those of her older sister, "Mommy, I'm sowwy she sobbed."

"I'm not your mommy," Nia cried uncontrollably, eagerly awaiting Nancy's return.

```
            Highland Park, Michigan
    Paradise Condominiums, Manchester Street
          7:05pm Eastern Standard Time
          2013 August 23, Friday
```

Over the last two years, the Henrik family found much needed financial stability through the will of Nia's left hand. During the summer after fifth grade, Nia submitted an illustration for a competition listed in the Highland Park Sun newspaper. Nine months later, she was a published illustrator.

On her way to ninth grade, it was a no brainer that she would take her talents to Louis Hampton High School of Arts in the neighboring city of Detroit. There, she could take her skills to the next level.

In her earlier years, it all seemed like a pipe dream. Especially after the school ushered in its tuition fee in the fall of 2005.

The tuition insertion was an executive decision voted on by the school's board of directors. It was the only way the school would survive after the state cut funds allocated to them.

Often during the 2004 school year, teachers and staff went weeks, even months without a paycheck. Their sudden financial burdens sometimes reflected in their performance on the clock. Disciplinary reports skyrocketed, and the quality of work was nothing like it was a year earlier.

Imposing tuition charges not only kept teachers happy financially, it restored the culture of the school, to one that nurtured success. Behavior problems simmered once high-quality projects decorated the walls of the school like old times. Students were able to see the fruits of their labor on a regular basis and pride was restored.

Many student composers from the Music Department were Intern Artists at Michigan Mu$ic Recordings with hundreds of record sales already on their resume.

The Art Department functioned like a business; from the atmosphere to its curriculum.

Visual Artists, Writers, and Editors made up the Art Department. Within the three wings of the building, they created several number one edition comic books and short stories.

Each season, they submitted one collective project to the Detroit Press Report and Highland Park Sun newspapers' quarterly competitions. They were sponsored by various publishing houses from all over the world. The students' works weren't always selected for publication, but the networking experiences were just as beneficial after graduation.

Admiring the artists before her in magazines and murals in Highland Park and Detroit, Nia couldn't wait to fine tune her skills. It was all she wanted to talk about.

"Come here, Aliya," Nia called from across the room.

Brushing the hair of her Lady Michigan look-alike model, Aliya placed her upright in the ShowTime Center replica arena. Postponing her reenactment of the 2013 LOTT Awards, Aliya whispered a pep talk to the other rubber plastic contestants, "I'll be back. Girls, you look stunning," she declared.

"Liya, did I tell you Louis Hampton High sent three students to Grandeur Fête in Paris? That's more than any school in the world. I'm going to be number four and you're going to be number five," Nia said fixing her little sister's hanging bangs.

"Me? I'm not an artist," Aliya said with her face in a ball of confusion.

"You're a model. You just don't know it yet. You look just like Gabby Powers when you walk around here like you're on a runway."

"Then why do you always make me stop?"

"I can only take so many fake smiles in one sitting. Besides, it's my job. Someone has to be tough on the twins when I'm gone, so take good notes. Mom lets you all do whatever you want but not me. I can't wait to go to college," Nia pouted.

"College? You haven't even started high school yet silly," Aliya reminded her.

"I know, but I still can't wait. I'm going to Peninsula State, Idlewild, or Michigan International University. Where do you want to go, Liya?"

"Umm... Peninsula State?" Aliya answered half certain, hoping to impress her older sister.

"Me too! Or maybe Idlewild. Too many people I know want to go to MIU."

"Even Trent?" Aliya smirked.

"Stop, Liya. I don't like him."

"That's not what I heard," Aliya snickered, anxious to spill the beans.

"You're nine. What could you have possibly heard about me?" Nia squinted.

"I didn't hear anything about you... but I heard Trent had a crush on you since you were little. Not much bigger than me!" she exclaimed dramatically.

"How do you know that!?" Nia blurted, attempting to cover her blushed cheeks with attitude.

"Trent was over my best friend Laurie's house with her big brother Dante. They were talking about the girls they liked from school and she heard Trent say he liked you since fifth grade."

Not knowing what to think, Nia figured she might as well get all the details while the topic was relevant. "He said that?"

"Umm hmm,"

"What else did he say?" Nia wondered.

"He said it was probably because you were the only person who could beat him up. Then they heard Laurie laugh and she got sent upstairs."

"He's always trying to be funny. Well, I don't like Trenton, not until he stops getting in so much trouble. He's too smart to be so bad."

"You used to be like that too. I've got the scars to prove it," Aliya said pulling up her pant leg.

"I'm soooooo sorry about that Liya, come here," rubbing her baby sister's scarred kneecaps; Nia patted, twisted, and turned until it produced laughter.

"That tickles," Aliya giggled.

"I'm going to miss you when I go up north," she said embracing her little sister.

"Good thing you still have four more years," Aliya replied, resting her head on Nia's yoga pants. The perfect material for a midday nap.

"I'm glad you two are having so much fun together," Nancy said opening the door to Nia's bedroom of the skyrise condominium. "Nia, I need you to watch the kids. I'm heading out. I'll be back before tomorrow morning. Try not to call unless it's an emergency," she reminded them on her way out the door.

"Mom, I told you last week I was going to a skating party tonight. This isn't fair!" Nia responded, drowning her eyes.

"You better watch your tone. Even though you help out with the bills for a change, I am still your mother. I shouldn't have to make you watch your brother and sisters. You should want to do it…" Nancy paused midsentence; heart broken by Nia's body language. "I'll make it up to you, Nia. Come here," she motioned for a hug.

"I ordered pizza. I know you all haven't eaten since you left school. It should be here shortly," Nancy assured them.

"Did you get one with chicken, cheddar, pineapples…"

"Jalapenos and barbecue sauce," Nancy said finishing Aliya's choice of toppings.

"Yes!" Aliya rejoiced.

"Love you girls. See you at breakfast, don't stay up too late," kissing her daughters goodbye, Nancy closed the door behind her. Nia and Aliya could hear the door alarm beep from the bedroom signaling Nancy's departure.

"Sorry Nia, I keep telling mommy I can watch the twins so you can go out sometimes, but she won't let me."

"It's okay, Liya. It's not your fault."

Pressing the elevator button for the ground floor, Nancy made it a point to check her voicemail before the night's festivities.

This message is for Nancy, Nancy Henrik. Hi, this is Maya Osman from Os House Publishing. We were calling to let you know that we decided to go in another direction with the illustrator position.

We have your number here and we're going to keep Nia's portfolio on file. We might be giving you a call back soon. Have a great day.

Bye-bye now.

"There she is," a voice acknowledged as the elevator doors opened to the lobby. "Kathy was on her way up if you didn't come down soon," Lynn joked, hugging Nancy as she exited the elevator.

"Sure was, I've been waiting for this book to become a play or a movie for years. You are *not* going to make us late," Katherine snapped with one hand, causing her purse to swing. "What's wrong, Nancy?" she frowned.

"Nothing, I'm fine. Nia was supposed to go to a skating party tonight. But somebody has to watch the kids," Nancy replied.

"Child please. You know how many skating parties I missed growing up because I had to babysit? Nia will be fine," Katherine assured her. "Think about how much you've missed through the years."

"You're right. It has felt good finally being able to get out the house," Nancy replied, feeling alive again. "That purse is cute, Kathy," she admired, rubbing the fine leather on the way out the lobby's golden doors.

"I got it from Bonita's. They're having a sale. I said I'd wait to go back. I need shoes and I knew you'd want to come with."

Friday 9:13pm, August 23, 2013

Dear Diary,

I can't wait until school starts! Two weeks and three days to be exact. I used to hate going back to school but now that I'm going to high school, I just can't wait! I'm so excited!

They sent us a packet in the mail with a list of everything we'll need. Markers, color pencils, pastels, chalk, and all that good stuff. Everything else will already be at the school. In the welcome letter it says, "Every artist should have their own tools."

Enough about school, I could go on and on all day. Guess who has a crush on me? Trent!!! Of all the girls in the school who talk about him all the time, he likes lil ole me!

What you really won't believe is who told me, Liya! The little doll came in handy after all. Liya's friend Laurie is Dante's sister, he's one of Trent's friends. Laurie was ear hustling when he said he liked me!

I had to pretend like I didn't care. I don't want Liya to think it's okay to like bad boys. If I can change, anybody can. Even my future husband, Trent. He has no excuse in my book. If he wants to be my husband, he has to change his ways and that's that!

I know none of this is new to you. It's probably already on half the pages of this book, but at least *now we know it's mutual. I just hope Liya doesn't already know all of this. I've caught her trying to read you twice already.*

Wait a minute, how did she even know I would care if Trent liked me? I bet that little girl already read you. I need answers.

Love ya,
Gotta go!

"Aliya!" Nia yelled across the hall from the doorway of her upstairs bedroom.

Highland Park, Michigan
15900 Woodward Avenue
Highland Park City High School
8:20am Eastern Standard Time
2013 October 23, Wednesday

The autumn chills bit abnormally hard, a little ahead of schedule, causing people to unpack their winter coats early. Walking inside the overcrowded hallway, the beeping sound ahead was a friendly reminder for Nia to empty her pockets before walking through the security metal detectors.

"Good morning, Mrs. Winters," Nia said, greeting the school's long-time security guard set to retire in a few years.

"Morning, sugar. You stay out of trouble today, Miss Ma'am," Mrs. Winters warmly warned.

"I will," Nia laughed, fixing the strap on her the purse.

"What's up freshman, I mean Nia?" a voice greeted from behind.

"I'm going to give you a pass today Trenton but only because it's early," Nia smiled, turning down the freshman hallway. "Nice haircut, big head."

"Thank you," Trenton grinned. "I haven't been down here all year," Trenton announced, admiring his old stomping grounds.

"Why are you here now? You're not a freshman anymore, Trenton. That was last year, honey. Give it up."

Did I just call him Honey! What was I thinking!?

"To see you, I mean… to ask you to stay out of trouble long enough to watch me hoop in Phys Ed., please?" Trenton bargained with a smile.

"Why would I want to watch you hoop?" she asked as Trenton appeared to be facing the aftershock from his first heartbreak in quite some time. "I'll stay out of trouble… if you stay out of trouble. That way I can *beat* you in fourth hour," Nia countered as her body rocked nervously, with her hands doing who knows what.

"You crack me up," Trenton laughed. "I don't get in trouble... in school. I'm a model student, sweetheart. Don't forget who inspired you to be valedictorian at Elmwood... and I didn't even go to Elmwood! But, because I won it in eighth grade, you knew you could do it too," Trenton boasted. "I paved the way for you, my lady."

"Whatever," Nia blushed.

"And I don't know what trouble you're talking about. I help the community a lot more than most people in the city," Trenton shrugged as a group of girls looked on with envy, watching the two interact from their lockers across the way.

"If you say so, Trenton... and okay, I'll stay out of trouble," the hug that sealed the deal didn't help the animosity growing around her. The clique of girls remained civilized until Trenton was well out of sight.

"You're not special," one girl shouted as the others laughed.

"She thinks she's cute now. Fix your new purse, *honey*. Your strap is looking like a Twizz-lerrr," another joked.

If I go over here and talk to these girls, everyone will tell me to "let it go." How come no one ever tells them to grow up? I'll ignore it this time. Four more hours... Nia closed her locker, turned her back and headed to class.

Morning classes went by with little resistance. Core subjects were her favorite; English, History, Math, and Writing at least. Science was a constant struggle, except Biology. It was surprisingly engaging to her.

Before afternoon classes, students had an hour to themselves for lunch and recreation. Seniors were the only group of students allowed to leave campus during the time span. All others were free to roam inside or around the three-acre campus.

Nia usually spent her time at the top level of the bleachers by the school fieldhouse, drawing or writing poetry.

<u>*Nobody Cares, 10-23-2013*</u>

Hypocrites, they are…

Who's "they"?

Who knows?

If you study history, you know how the story goes.

Nobody cares…

We all know the problem is really the posers who show fake love but stunt your growth in reality.

We're all shrinking unless you're thinking.

Maybe that's just me.

Spirit of a butterfly with the sting of the bee. Because of Muhammad Ali, I know even when nobody cares…

I'll still be The Greatest.

By Nia Henrik 12:10pm

Nia used the remainder of her time finishing a picture she drew for an ad in the Highland Park Sun newspaper.

Contests

&

Competitions...

Become an Illustrator!

Add us on social media @LOTT48203

OR

Send a 10-picture portfolio to
Management@LOTT48203.com

Candidates will be contacted to begin production
for upcoming projects.

Good luck!

With time ticking away, Nia carefully packed up her poems and newspaper clips. As she exited the bleachers, she could see trouble brewing ahead of her like a hot pot of fresh ground coffee at Sandy's.

> *Who sits by themselves all the time?*
> **Nia!**
> *The biggest weirdo in grade-9*
> **Nia!**
> *She'll fight anybody at the drop of a dime...*
> **Nia!**
> *I won't be surprised if we can't finish this rhyme.*
> *When Nia's coming for you, you can run but you can't hide.*
> **Whooooo!**
> **Nooo Nia!**

The girls laughed, cheering on from the landing area. The clap-stomp routine was so precise, it ignited a loud, echoing applause from above. "That was good girls, really good. Bernice, I saw you trip back there, be careful next time, toots. Somebody who cares might see you," Nia said walking past the clique of girls and back to class.

1 hour, 10 minutes

Highland Park City High School Gymnasium
15900 Woodward Avenue
1:30pm Eastern Standard Time
2013 October 23, Wednesday

Opening her gym locker for the first time in too long, Nia removed a pair of damp, smelly gym shoes.

As a member of the school's basketball and cross-country team, she had access to her practice locker as well. Having tossed the soiled gym shoes into the equipment manager's rubber bin, Nia grabbed a fresh set of school gear and footwear from locker fourteen.

Making her way back to physical education class, the other girls awaited her arrival like a city bus. "Sorry Trent didn't make it," Cassandra teased with a smile.

"What are you talking about?" Nia asked, fixing the front of her t shirt."

"Your little basketball date. Trent isn't here. He left campus again to eat lunch with the seniors. He's probably suspended by now. Looks like you combed your hair for nothing today," Cassandra laughed reaching inside Nia's locker.

"You're going to smell nastier than that locker of yours after gym without this," Cassandra plotted, winding her arm back before tossing Nia's sweater with the football team's dirty laundry.

"I can't believe you," Nia said as she jumped on top of the Cassandra in the middle of the aisle way. The two kicked and clawed for half a minute before being separated by the locker room attendant.

I should have done this earlier. I knew he wouldn't come.

Nia waited for the school's security guard on the bench outside the gymnasium. Mrs. Winters motioned for the girls as Nia locked eyes with a young man walking innocently to the boy's locker room, eating a bag of salted almonds.

His black hat and navy jacket were a giveaway that he recently reentered the building. Lengthening his stride, holding a royal blue duffle bag, he left the scene as quickly as he came.

"Mr. Booker," Mrs. Winters called out as the girls giggled behind her.

"Commme baaack," she dragged out theatrically.

"You're coming with us too, sir. You're not a senior yet young man. We've been looking for you for almost an hour," Mrs. Winters finished, pointing to the end of the line with the antenna of her two-way radio.

Frowning at the girls, Trenton's eyebrows nearly touched by the time he got in line. Looking at Nia last, she dropped her head knowing exactly what he wanted to say.

You couldn't wait 10 more minutes?

"Oops," she whispered as they left for the Principal's Office.

```
                Highland Park, Michigan
                     North Avenue
             11:53pm Eastern Standard Time
              2013 October 23, Wednesday
```

10/23/2013

Dear Detective Dr. Rydon Tyme,

At this point, I think the only reason I still write you is because it's therapeutic. Whenever this time rolls around, things are either going really good or really bad. This is one of the years when things are going really bad.

I won a $10,000 contest the summer before sixth grade. They called it a contest, but it was really just a contract. The newspapers here have competitions for artists and writers all the time.

The winners get a fully, guaranteed contract with whatever publishing house that sponsors the competition. After I won the contest, I had to draw 10 illustrations a year, for 2 years. It was the hardest thing I ever had to do. They were never satisfied!

I cried so many times. It made me a better artist, that's for sure. My first project, they asked what my favorite medium was. I said watercolor.

They had me redo my first illustration 3 times, 3 different ways before saying, "How about watercolor?" I did it and they loved it. "We've never seen watercolor look so realistic," they kept saying.

Mama said she wanted a fresh start after my contract was up, so she sold the house on Grand Street. She was able to get triple the price she paid with all the renovations.

We have a lot of houses. My granddaddy bought a bunch of them during the Great Recession after the housing market crashed. You could buy a house for a few hundred dollars. Still can in some places.

Papa has been fixing up houses since my daddy was little. Now he's retired. He still works on his houses and will sell or rent them out. I had him buy me a house with some money I saved from commissions a couple years ago. Fixing it up was our project together. He said it was the least he could do for raising a knuckleheaded son.

Wait, wait, wait, I have to pause this letter Dr. Tyme. We were neighbors for a little over a year! Our Condo was right under your penthouse. We didn't request it or anything, it just happened that way.

Your mail would come down to our place sometimes and we'd send it back to the mailroom. I kept hoping I'd see you on the elevator one day, but it never happened. You never came!

I don't know why I always got so upset about it. You don't owe us anything. I know you don't care anymore. Nobody cares, not even my mama.

You know why we're not neighbors anymore Dr. Tyme? My mama, that's why!

After my contract expired a little while ago, I had a lot of extra time and I didn't like it. I started researching ways to make money as a published artist. That's when I started selling my work at auctions, easy money.

I had already made enough money to cover my tuition for all four years at Louis Hampton High School of Arts with my contract. I used $8,000 for tuition. I gave mama $1,000 and I had her get me a savings bond for a $1,000.

Since I'm under 18, mama had control over the money. I'd get gifts but never any money. September came around and mama didn't have any money either. Not tuition money or my savings bond. She couldn't show much of anything. Just a lot of clothes, shoes, some jewelry, purses, and crumbled up receipts.

We met a lot of fancy people at my art shows and auctions that we'd go to. Sometimes my work sold, sometimes it didn't. But either way, before we left, mama would end up laughing it up the media and some high rollers, planning trips, vacations, and events on the fly.

She said she thought I'd get another big contract to cover the cost for my tuition before school started. How do you spend $9,000 that isn't yours! Not to mention the other $45,000 from the Grand Street sale.

Come to find out we were renting the condo the entire time. While she was out in Hollywood, LA, and Las Vegas every weekend, spending all our money. Pretending to be rich on the West Coast, "Networking" she called it.

If she would've paid the deposit with the money from the house on Grand Street, the condo would almost ours to keep by now! $10,000 wasn't enough???

I guess she needed all $55,000 dollars to keep up with people who don't even care about her. If I'm lying, where are they now? She spent all that money in a year Dr. Tyme! 1 year! It's not fair.

All of that is the reason I have to attend Highland Park City High. Along with every girl I ever fought growing up. There isn't a high school in Highland Park like Elmwood. So after we graduate from eighth grade, we all meet up at HP City High.

I give Elmwood credit for that. We learned a lot of stuff there that they don't teach here, even in high school. We were learning about stocks and bonds in the seventh grade. By the time we got to eighth grade, we were learning about real estate and grant writing.

I've been in three fights already this year. Two were during the first week of school. All three were with girls I beat up at Elmwood when we were in elementary school.

I don't like fighting anymore, Dr. Tyme. I'm trying to be more like Aliya. A nine year old? I know right.

But she always tells me to "Act like a lady," but sometimes they won't let me.

You're probably thinking 'If you fought three times, how were you not suspended?' It's 2013, Dr. Tyme. We have empty back hallways these days but if we get caught, it's a three, five, or ten-day suspension.

I blame Kimani for the way that I act. We fought a lot growing up. I knew it would come out of me again one day.

I'm not talking about fighting each other either. We fought people from other neighborhoods, together. He was always getting us in trouble. Especially after basketball games because he's a jokester and sometimes he goes too far.

He's a senior now at the High School for Higher Learning. The starting pitcher for the Heroes and the school's first small forward ever. He's 6'6 now. I'm so proud of him.

The Heroes finally have a full sports program. Lucky McWallace and Aaron Homer sponsored the entire athletic department after they were drafted to play pro ball last June.

The basketball team looked really good this summer. They almost beat my school in a scrimmage. If he works hard enough, he might get an offer from MIU like he's always dreamed of.

After all that went down with mama, I moved out and into my house. The one me and Papa fixed up on North Ave. I'm an emancipated minor now.

Technically I'm too young. But because so much money was involved, I was able to petition the court. Having a house already and being able to save $1,000 since my contract expired made me look pretty responsible. The judge said even with all of that, he only granted my request because I turn 16 this year.

I wanted to take Liya with me but it wasn't happening. I was barely able to move out myself. She has a room here though and she spends the night enough to think she lived here.

I'll get another illustrator deal one day. Until then $100 here, $50 there, $250 every now and then is how I keep the lights on.

If you ever come back, our house is the one with the big flag on the porch, like the one from the book "Headed West". You ever read that book before? They just made it into a play. I'm rambling now.

Well, Dr. Tyme, it's bedtime. Goodnight!

Love you always and still your biggest fan,
Nia

P.S. That gives me an idea of this year's picture. It's going to be of me sleeping. Why? I don't know, Dr. Tyme. I don't argue with my visions; I just bring them to life.

```
Highland Park City High School
      15900 Woodward Avenue
 1:45pm Eastern Standard Time
   2015 October 23, Friday
```

October 23, 2015

Dear Dr. Tyme,

Well, Dr. Tyme, this is almost the end of the road between you and me. I first wrote you back in first grade. Kimani had a Royal Freeze comic book and you were in the book! You've been my favorite superhero ever since because I always thought you were real. Now, I don't know what to think. Were you a person or a character? Both? I'm so confused???

When I first started writing you, I thought I'd do it forever. Then around ninth or tenth grade, I said the last thing I would send you, were tickets to my graduation.

If you don't come, it will bring closure to this mystery and I will accept that you passed away years ago like everyone says.

I also have an early invite for you to see me off for prom. Trent asked me last week! Who's Trent? I know right. Sorry Dr. Tyme. Trent is my boyfriend of seven days now.

I'd LOVE it if you came to see us off May 3, 2016 at 6:30 p.m. Aliya just told me to ask if you could bring Gabby Powers with you.

I don't want to tell you how I've been doing socially. I know you wouldn't be too proud. My grades are really good though! I have a 3.4 cumulative grade point average to start off our Jr. year. I'm going to get a 4.0 this card marking, watch me.

I try to keep myself busy in class to stay out of trouble. Like writing this letter for example. We're in Mrs. Jameson's fifth hour for Social Studies and I'm bored out of my mind. She gives us these fifth grade worksheets that we finish in ten minutes, then she has the nerve to get mad when everyone starts talking.

I stay out of detention by working on commissions after finishing my "work." People say Mrs. Jameson used to be a great teacher back in the day. "One of the best," they always say. Looks like she gave up to me. The way we act up, I'd be tired too.

Since this is my second to last time writing you, I'm going to ask two questions before I go.

1. Is the Secret 7 real?

2. Why did you disappear off the grid like that?

I doubt you'll answer either but at least I tried. We still live on North Ave. just look for the flag whenever you make it back.

Rest in peace, Dr. Tyme. Love you always,
Nia

P.S. This year's picture will be one of a kind. You can bet on that! I might have to put us, (you and I) on the Great Pyramids or somewhere in Saint-Domingue. Who knows?

The bell signaling the last hour of the day sounded promptly at 1:45 p.m. It couldn't have come with better timing. Students were boiling over with frustration left and right. Fights were breaking out all over the building, sending the security staff up and down the stairwells from the cafeteria to the gymnasium.

Nia was able to avoid her foes and she preferred to keep it that way as she headed up the back stairwell to the 3rd floor. Entering room *314*, Nia went straight to her favorite seat in the far corner, under the old television by the exit door.

Whisking away at her latest masterpiece, her concentration was snapped as a wad of paper hit her pencil. The slight bump of force caused a permanent error on a once flawless canvas. With her face in a ball resembling the crumbled paper falling next to her, Nia quickly surveyed the class for the culprit.

Narrowing down the choices to two people, she figured it had to be the new girl Irena or her newfound best friend, Cassandra. Ready to set the tone with an unfamiliar face and one she had seen too many times; Nia was smacked with another paper ball. Hitting her in the center of the forehead.

Realizing the toss came from friendly fire, her facial expression changed quicker than a model on the runway. "You can't play like that TJ. You almost got those two in trouble," she said pointing at the young ladies laughing at their own jokes, sitting against the wall.

"What did I tell you about fighting so much?" Trenton asked.

"Don't do it," Nia answered, hiding her blushed cheeks with the palms of her hands.

"You're too pretty to be fighting," Trenton said, moving her hands away from her brown sugar-colored cheeks.

"So, what's your excuse, handsome?" Nia wondered as they held hands.

"I'm a soldier," he laughed. "I'm supposed to fight. Not to mention, anybody I've ever had to wreck, had it coming."

"What about Brian, who lived down the street from me?"

"That was third grade Nia. You can't keep bringing up old stuff."

The victims of puppy love continued their conversation as if they had nothing to do or nowhere to go. "Mr. Booker, what are you doing in the hallway and Miss Henrik, why aren't you in a seat," Mrs. Winters asked, standing directly behind Trenton in the hallway.

As aware as he may have been in the neighborhood, he never sensed her presence around the corner. "Mrs. Winters, I was just going to the bathroom," he said holding up an expired hall pass.

"This was written forty minutes ago, Mr. Booker. Why would you do something like this during a hall sweep? You two told me you'd have a better day than what you've shown. I'm very disappointed in the both of you," Mrs. Winters reminded them as they departed.

Frustrated from such a busy day, a tear dropped undetected from the corner wrinkle of Mrs. Winters' eye. Quickly regaining her composure with the swipe of her thumb, she lectured the group of students caught with expired hall passes the entire walk to the office.

"Say bye, Mr. Booker," Mrs. Winters reasoned, fixing her eye glasses.

Trenton and Nia had a highly publicized relationship. The feelings they shared for each other formed outside of school. They lived a few streets away from each other, but Trenton frequently visited friends in Nia's neighborhood.

Now that the two were school mates for the first time since Nia was in kindergarten, they were destined to be high school sweethearts. "See you later, Nia," Trenton said with his head hung.

"Later as in Tuesday," Mrs. Winters warned, causing Trenton's jaw to drop. "Unless you see her this weekend, because you'll be out Monday. That's for certain young sir."

"Come on, Mrs. Winters!" Trenton shouted in anguish. "I have Senioritis. You know that's a diagnosed illness, right?"

"Mr. Booker, Mr. Booker..." Mrs. Winters said shaking her head. "You've had *senioritis* since you were a freshman. I'll let your teacher decide," Mrs. Winters said, escorting him back to class, while Nia stared into the abyss.

After school, Trenton, Calvin, Victor, Stanley, and the other boys waited under the trees in the courtyard for the rest of the crew. One of the boys was obviously a little more distraught than the others.

Walking pass the group of boys, Cassandra Anderson had to see what the problem was. "Hey TJ, what's wrong?" she asked pressing her body against his.

"What's up Cassie? I'll be alright," Trenton answered shortly, knowing his girlfriend wouldn't approve of their after school rendezvous.

"Doesn't look like it," she said smacking her glossed lips.

The other boys looked on under the tree as their friend continued to dig himself into a hole big enough for a treasure chest. "What do you think Nia will do if she sees this?" Victor whispered to Stan.

"If we're talking about the same, Nia, we might witness World War III," they laughed.

Standing strong, holding his hands, it was obvious Trenton wasn't interested in what was in front of him. "How come you never hug me anymore, TJ?" Cassandra asked with her arms around his waist, looking deep into his dark brown eyes.

"You know I have girlfriend, and we both know she would trip if she saw you all over me like this," Trenton answered.

"You've changed," Cassandra said with an attitude, leaving a frown on her nose and brow. Distancing herself from Trenton, Cassandra headed down the stairs of the courtyard, toward Woodward Avenue.

"You see what I have to go through V? No matter what I do, I'm always the bad guy. You better keep Francine happy," Trenton warned, pointing at Victor.

"I'm trying," Victor laughed, as they slapped hands.

The boys waited almost an hour before realizing they had yet to depart. "Has anyone seen Nia?" Trenton asked the boys around him with no luck.

"Nope."

"Earlier."

"Not since third hour," they all answered.

```
        Highland Park, Michigan
      Sandy's Burgers and Breakfast
      3:04pm Eastern Standard Time
         2015 October 23, Friday
```

Nia sat at the back table next to the window, nursing hunger pains with her friends. As they waited for their food to arrive, in walked trouble through the side door.

"Really, let me see?" Cassandra said to Irena, as she and the other girls took their spots in line. "Uhn uhnn, I can't believe they posted that. Whose page is this?"

"Ju'Dario," Denise said taking a menu from the counter.

"I should have known. He's always starting rumors, especially about TJ. I wish it was something to spread this time. He's over me," Cassandra said as her eyes began to water. "He wouldn't hug me, and his eyes. He looked at me like he hated me. What did I do to him?"

"Awww Cassie, don't cry. Here," Roslyn said handing Cassandra a napkin from the dispenser. "Don't let him make you cry girl. If he wants to be with Nia, let him be with Nia."

Nia was oblivious to the conversation ahead of her until hearing her name a second time. Roslyn had a very distinct voice that could be heard across any room no matter the size. With or without a microphone. "Did you hear Roslyn say my name?" Nia asked.

"I didn't hear anything. I just want my food. You know I'm a fat," Francine answered, watching the overworked waitresses pass out plates like a deck of cards at every table but theirs.

"I heard Trent's name but not yours," Rhonda answered, squeezing a lemon slice over her glass of ice water.

"I guess I'll let it slide since your best friend is crying and what not," Nia said to her elbow partner.

"She's not my best friend but that is my girl. Cass isn't too bad once you get to know her," Simone said defending a close friend on her way out of the booth. "I'll go check on our food."

There were students everywhere and they didn't hesitate to announce their presence.

Hey Simone, can I have a hug?
Do you want to go to the mall with me this weekend, and to the movies?
They only came up to you because I told them I'd ask you out first.

The boys all said, shooting their best shots. Annoyed by it all, Simone stood silently in line, waiting her turn all over again.

"Welcome to Sandy's. How can I help you?" asked the cashier in training.

"May I speak to the Manager?" Simone said, finally being acknowledged.

A woman restocking the freezers nearby took the helm upon request. "Yes ma'am, I'm Loraine. How can I help?" she asked with a smile.

"Hi Loraine, we've been waiting on our food for a long time, almost an hour now. At least it feels like it. We stood in line once already and now I have to ignore these little boys with short memories. Except I'm alone this time.

"In school, they do things like hit you with paper balls and airplanes like fourth graders. Then when the bell rings, all of sudden they want to be nice to you and go out on dates. I shouldn't have to go through all of this for food, how much longer Ms. Loraine?"

"I'm sorry sweetie," Loraine responded. "We've been really busy and understaffed lately. If you know anyone who may want a job with college scholarship opportunities, tell them to apply online and reference me," Loraine said handing Simone her business card.

"It should be no longer than another five to seven minutes. Would you like some dessert for your table, free of charge?"

Reaching for the business card, Simone accepted her kind gesture as well. "Thank you. I know a few people who need a job, like one, two, and three," Simone said, pointing at the boys behind her.

"We'll take a Strawberry Cheesecake with a pint of vanilla pound cake ice cream, thank you."

"No problem. We'll bring it to you at your request, enjoy," Loraine smiled.

Simone was never the type to let her friend's disagreements interfere with her personal relations. She was a social butterfly, beloved by most her peers. "What's wrong, Cass?" she asked, making a pit stop on the way to her seat.

"Hey Mo, nothing I'm fine… no, I'm not," she said, breaking down into Simone's arms.

"Cassandra is doing the most right now," Nia said looking on from afar.

"I wonder what happened," Francine wondered.

"Simone will tell us when she gets back," Nia replied reading a text from Trenton.

Are you still at school?
Hello to you too Trenton. No, we're at Sandy's, you coming?
Lol @ Trenton, my bad. I meant… What's up sweetie?
You're learning
Lol keep schooling me lady ma'am. Can you do me a huuuuuge favor?
What's up?
Could you order a beef gravy burger for me?
Lol yes. I thought it was something serious
That was serious lol we're otw
K

"We," Nia giggled aloud, "I always forget he never travels alone."

"What are you talking about girl?" Francine asked.

"Trent is on his way with who knows how many people."

"I hope Stan is one of them," Rhonda blushed. "He's so cute and don't get me started on that bald head and he's a brace face too."

With girl talk present and at large, social media posts became Nia's next topic of discussion. "Felicity and Roxanne are so pretty."

"Who are they?" Rhonda wondered.

"Victor's sisters, everybody thinks they're twins but Roxanne is a senior and Felicity is a junior," she answered, handing away her phone.

"Oh, yeah, they're beautiful and that bag is too cute," Rhonda praised. Cycling through the pictures and videos posted on Nia's *Watcherz* profile, Rhonda refreshed the screen to view the most recent posts.

"I'm going through your *Watched List* like this is my phone," Rhonda said as her thumb swiped the screen. The most recent post triggered a reaction, broadcasting live on Rhonda's face.

"What?" Nia asked taking back her phone. "Really," she said shaking her head, not knowing how to respond.

"Maybe it's not what it looks like?" Rhonda suggested.

"What does it look like?" Nia quickly replied.

"Like TJ and Cassie are an item," she mumbled, scratching a head that did not itch.

The conversation between Cassandra and Trenton went viral on *Watcherz* in a moment's time, "That's what I thought too. Maybe it's old right?" Nia asked, giving Trenton the benefit of the doubt.

"Not unless she wore the same outfit," Francine chimed in, biting through a chip of ice.

Trenton and Cassandra became boyfriend and girlfriend during the summer after eighth grade. They met during the citywide celebration for students getting ready to enter high school. Many laughs and trips to the Detroit River later, they were the new favorites to win class couple, four years early.

Drama got the best of them as freshmen, leading to their break-up during a rocky summer before their sophomore year. Insert Nia, the innocent freshman from Elmwood Academy ignorant to it all.

Over the years Cassandra and Nia developed a love-hate relationship for one another and decided it would be best to stay out of each other's way. Salted tears were the only thing that kept the peace in Sandy's Burgers and Breakfast.

"I want to go over there so bad right now, but she looks so pathetic," Nia said as Simone returned to the table. "What's wrong with her?"

"I don't know she didn't say," Simone replied.

"It's like that now, Simone? I already know. All you had to say was, you didn't want to tell me," Nia said in a rage, sliding her phone across the table.

"This is from today?" Simone asked, looking at the screen.

"Don't act dumb, Simone. I thought we were friends and you weren't even going to tell me that Sandra was all hugged up with my man?"

"Nia, you need help. Cass didn't tell me anything. When have I ever lied to you?" Gathering her belongings, she made one last remark. "They were right about you. You'd fight a clock just because it has hands. Bye Francine, Rhonda, hmmph…" she said, flipping her hair away from Nia as she walked out.

"What's up, Simone?" Trenton said entering the diner.

"Oh, be quiet," she uttered as the boys walked by.

"What did I do? Trent said looking in Calvin's direction.

"I don't know but Nia has the same look," Calvin said, trying his hardest not to draw attention to themselves.

Taking a seat next to Nia in the booth, Trenton looked deep into Nia's eyes, "You should make that face more often, I love the way the light hits the wrinkle between your eyes. Makes me want to yell, *Hurt me! Hurt me!* Like the Fresh Prince on that one episode."

"You make me so sick!" Nia laughed against her will, "Just because I'm smiling, doesn't mean I'm not mad at you."

"What are you talking about?" Trenton wondered, confused from it all.

"This," she said tossing her phone in the air.

Instantly, all Trenton could do was laugh, "That's what this is about? When you find out what really happened, you're going to feel bad about the way you're treating me."

"Whatever Trenton," she said leaving the table and the restaurant all together.

"Nia," Trenton called out.

While Trenton was looking around, trying to figure out what was going on. Nia was already in the back of a taxi, on her way home.

"What just happened?" Trenton asked, as the other girls boxed their food to go. Smirking the whole time, the girls sought after their heartbroken friend.

"You know what happened," one said on the way out as the door slammed.

Sitting alone in the same booth his girlfriend just departed, Trenton rested his head in his hands. Taking a seat next to him was the person responsible for it all. "Is she mad at you? Didn't look like she wanted to hear what you had to say," Cassandra said with bloodshot eyes.

"I'm making everybody cry today, I see," Trenton said shaking his head.

"I always heard you out when we had our problems and I never left you. I'll always be by your side."

Resting her head on his shoulder, Trenton looked at her with a blank stare, "It's over Cassandra, you know that," he responded, biting into his beef gravy burger.

After a phone call with friends, Nia returned ready to apologize. Only to leave heartbroken once again, by her best friend. "He doesn't care either," she said, seeing their conversation transpire from the front window of the establishment.

Nia continued to cry, waving her hand for the Downtown-Jefferson Big Bus. The soothing waves of the Detroit River called her name from miles away. The sun was shining, and the winds sent waters crashing a steady half note. Perfectly drowning out her cries.

Cars lined the block on both sides of the street. Normally, half of them would have been ticketed and or towed for illegal parking. On this particular day, some law enforcement officers would have been guilty themselves.

Prom season was one of the city's most festive events. Seniors all over town posed for the flashing lights, tablets, and camera phones, looking at whoever called their name, cheeks frozen with picture perfect smiles.

However, one of its participants wasn't in the mood to celebrate. "I can't believe I let you talk me into this, Liya. I should've broken this off a long time ago," Nia frowned from her grandmother's old make up chair.

"Me, me, I, I, me, me, me; this is bigger than you, Nia," Aliya reminded her, emphasizing her point with the tip of her fingernail. "Gabby Powers is coming."

"I told you not to get your hopes up, Liya. I've been writing Dr. Tyme since I was younger than you and he's never replied."

Choosing to protect her sister's innocence, Nia left the topic alone. At her age, she too thought she controlled the universe and its happenings, so long as she held tight to her faith, no matter how naïve she may have sounded.

"That's because you're bad sometimes. I wouldn't come see you either if I were a celebrity," Aliya laughed, recklessly waving her eyeshadow brush.

"Watch that thing," Nia chuckled, popping her leg with an open hand.

"I'm serious. Since Dr. Tyme told Gabby Powers that I wanted to see her in your letter, he doesn't have a choice. She's my best friend. I never told you that? You can thank me now," Aliya said finishing her sister's mascara.

As the pageant queen of the family, Aliya was honored when asked to be Nia's makeup artist for the big day. "Smile, Nia. You're messing up my work."

"You happy now?" Nia replied, with unnaturally parted lips.

"No," Aliya pouted, handing Nia a mirror as the phone rang.

Ring, ring, ring!

The opened door allowed the girls to know right away who it was, based off their mother's mood change. Her laughter could be heard from the hallway landline telephone.

"Hey, TJ. How's your mom?" Nancy answered excitedly; the way Nia used to. "Okay. I'll let her know. See you in a little bit, bye-bye."

Knocking on the door before entering the room, Nancy was at a loss for words the moment she saw Nia's face. "Wow. Nia, you look beautiful. Aliya you did a great job even though she looks so mean.

"Cheer up, Nia Pia. TJ is on his way, the family is downstairs and the whole neighborhood is here to see you off."

Removing the cape that covered her dress, Nia tried making the most of a sour situation. "You said yourself that you overreacted," Nancy said, hoping to ease the pain.

"I know I did but as soon as we broke up, who does he get spotted at the movies with? Cassandra. It's never going to be over between those two. No matter how much he pretends to care about me."

"You know I understand where you're coming from and you probably won't like what I'm going to say, but I'll say it anyway. When you two were together, it didn't look like he was pretending to me."

"I just don't want to have to compete with anybody mom."

"And you shouldn't have to. What I'm trying to tell you is that I don't think you had any competition. These enemies you've been creating all these years are mostly mental. That boy loves you Nia, don't let him get away. You might regret it later," she said, catching her daughter's tear and saving her makeup.

Aliya wiped sweat from her own forehead, witnessing the emotional wreck in front of her. "It's too late, mom. He likes a girl from Victory High now. That's really why I don't want to go but Aliya's making me."

"If you were able to forgive me after all that we went through, maybe he should get a second chance too," Nancy said, reminiscing on the past.

"That's different, you're my mom. I wouldn't be here if it wasn't for you. Trent doesn't know what he wants right now, am I supposed to wait around until he does?"

"I hear you. I still think you might thank Liya at your wedding one day, for *making* you go tonight, you never know. Life is funny like that," Nancy said as a grin crept onto Nia's face.

"I hope that's not the last smile of the night or you're going to upset a lot of folks downstairs. Mr. Bright is here. He came not too long before TJ called."

"Really!?" Nia exclaimed. "I haven't seen him since Jr. High."

"I know. He told us. He said you forgot all about your elementary school teachers once you got to high school."

"Uh oh," she laughed. "I told him I'd come back once a year until I graduated college when I was little."

Walking down the stairway with her nude leather heels in hand, Nia took a seat on the second step to fasten her footwear. Entering through the kitchen door, Trenton eased to a knee to lend her a hand. "I got it," he said sliding her foot into her shoes.

"That's the first time I've seen you smile at me in months," he said reaching for her hand.

"I'm not smiling," she giggled as a flash lit up the hallway.

"Yes, you were," Aliya said waving her picture, waiting for it to develop.

"Good shot, kid. Here, buy yourself something nice," Trenton said slipping the photographer a ten dollar bill."

"Thanks!"

The people gathered on the front lawn seemed like they were witnessing a royal wedding. They were breaking their necks for a view at one of the hottest couples in the neighborhood.

"Nia go take a picture by the limo," Nancy instructed, pointing to the street.

After nearly twenty minutes of different poses and positions, Nia noticed Cassandra and Desmond caught Trenton's attention with their photoshoot across the street. Everything inside her believed Cassandra only accepted Desmond's invitation because he stayed so close to Nia.

Then Nancy's voice rang like a snoozed alarm: *These enemies you've been creating all these years are mostly mental…*

"Trenton," she called.

"You look amazing," he said, snapping back to reality.

"Don't even try it," she said, sporting her favorite nose wrinkle.

"I came a long way, Nia. The least you could do is smile," one voice called from the crowd.

"Sorry, Uncle Lou," she apologized, grinning her way back into high spirits.

"That wasn't me, baby girl," Uncle Lou chuckled with the crowd.

Standing behind Uncle Lou was a man wearing all white with matching hair. His uniquely crafted cane, glistening gold, and tinted eyewear brought Nia an epiphany.

"Dr. Tyme!"

May 7, 2016

My Dearest Gabby Powers,

Hey best friend? I hope you're having fun in Jerusalem. When you get back, you have to invite me to see you. It's your turn now that you've visited me. Thanks for coming by the way. I told Nia you all would come this whole time, but she didn't believe me. Ever since she met Dr. Donny, she's been acting like a new person. She let us move in and everything.

You look stunning for your age, darling. What do you use for your skin? And your hair, I can't wait for my hair to turn salt and pepper. Don't get me started on that dress, sweetie. Can you have one made for me? I'll be in LOTT's Little Leaders Talent Showcase in the fall. That'd be grand if I had it before then!

Coming in third last year made me work even harder. With the sound of my piccolo and that dress, I can't lose. After I win, I'll bring my trophy and play my piccolo for you and your family.

I'm glad you told me to make Nia go to the prom. If she didn't meet Dr. Donny this year, I think she would act different than she does now. She was back to being the old Nia, starting fights and staying in trouble.

This girl in my class named Ellen has a sister Nia's age. Nia got into a fight with Ellen's big sister at her school and Ellen stopped being my friend after that. She said she didn't want to stop being my friend. She said her mom told her to.

It was great finally getting to meet you. I can't believe you let me braid your hair. Send me pictures when you take them down. Your curls are going to be on fleek. Can't wait to hear from you!

Love,
Aliya Henrik

June 14, 2016

Madam Aliya Henrik,

As always it is so delightful to hear from you. We are having a ball here in Israel. So much so, Ry is thinking about moving here for good. This man moves more than the ocean levels, Honey Child. Wherever he lies his hat is his home. Then he says what he always says when he wants to stay a little longer, "We're World Citizens for a reason, cutie. We might as well stick around." Then he pinches my cheeks. That man of mine.

Whenever he says that, I know I better find something I like about wherever we are because it's no telling how long we'll be there. He's getting older, so he says things twice now. That's when you know he's serious. I'm not yet 90, so that explains the salt and pepper color. Don't you dare rush for this look. You keep flipping those brown locks, Toots. As for my skin, honey and olive oil are your friends unless you're allergic. Then not so much.

You most absolutely, positively, even if it's Sunday, certainly can have this dress. Then guess what? We're going to get you a photo shoot with the Little Dolls Boutique. That'd be right on time for their line of summer dresses. How does that sound? I'll have my stylist set it up as soon as we get back to ground level.

I'm writing you on our break. We're hiking through the mountains, as usual. He's the historian, yet I always end up on these random expeditions. Does that make me a historian too? Don't mind me, Sugar; I'm just thinking to myself.

Let's get back to you Miss Missy. I'm glad you were able to get Nia to the prom. Once I realized your sister was the little girl whose pictures decorate our cabin in Northern Michigan, I had to make sure he came with. So, you are very welcome, Honey.

Ry started reading Nia's letters maybe three to four years ago. Then he dug up all her old mail and sent her a few things, but she always sent them back. Then he told me Nia thought he passed away and began using him to vent her frustrations.

He was so confused about all of that. When he told me you invited me, I finally put two and two together. I guess it's a good thing I'm not the Detective.

Tell Nia she got her wish. Ry just told me he's going to have a sit-down interview with LOTT Magazine, presenting all our new findings to the world. To "set the record straight" whatever that means. He's finally coming out from under his rock! I can't tell you how long I've been dying to get back to work with the girls on the runway.

Meeting you was my pleasure. You can braid my hair anytime and the curls were definitely on fleek, Sweetie. I'll get those pictures in the mail and tickets for you and your family to visit us during your winter break if it's okay with your mother and sister. Good luck in the contest!

Your best friend,
Gabriella "Gabby Powers" Tyme

Bad Move

Preview

```
Mackinac Island, Michigan
4:27pm Eastern Standard Time
1968 February 9, Friday
```

Skating in the midst of a winter wonderland, courtesy of Mother Michigan, Rydon and Gabriella Tyme were thoroughly enjoying their unexpected getaway. The couple created separate bank accounts for emergencies and opportunities. The accounts were used to finance what Rydon referred to as the E's and O's of life.

When things got rough, they withdrew funds from their emergency account. Opportunity seemed to strike equally as often, so there was an account for that as well.

Zipping atop Lake Huron, the couple arrived at 716 Haji Hill, a 987-foot hilly terrain that towered over the lands of Mighty Michigan.

Rydon diversified himself throughout his forty two years. He didn't restrict himself to stereotypes or societal norms. He did things that brought him happiness, willing to try almost anything once.

His wife, Gabriella, was the same way and together, they made the world their playground. Sitting on the edge of the frozen pier, Rydon removed the icy skates from Gabriella's toasty tots. Briefly massaging and replacing them with snow boots.

"That feels so good. I promise, you read my mind," Gabriella giggled.

The two never lost lust for each other since the day they locked eyes. They were perfect for one another. Rydon Tyme was the most romantic man she'd ever met and fortunately for her, she was stuck with him for life.

He was her Prince Charming in the flesh, always leaving her blushing like a twenty year old. "Ry, how far did we just ice skate?" Gabriella asked, resting her body weight on her heavily padded elbows.

"At least a mile, maybe two," Rydon replied.

The Tyme's were self-employed, adventurous, and loved to travel. They set their own office hours, essentially writing their own rules. The Mackinac Island getaway was much needed and appreciated.

"You want to warm up, or go snowboarding with me?" Rydon asked.

Rydon enjoyed Haji Hill most; it was his favorite of all their getaways. In the summer, all of the action was on the east side of the hill, which featured a water slide leading right into Lake Huron. During the wintertime, the hill hosted many races down its snowy slope to the lodge at the bottom.

Long ago, the Tyme family built a house atop Haji Hill, overlooking the Lower Peninsula of Michigan. The cabin brought Rydon back to reality after his most mentally taxing cases as a public defender. His service to the community gave them high quality representation at the expense of his emotional stability.

What bothered him most was the level of corruption he witnessed during his time as a detective and part time public defender. The more he learned, the more frustrated he became. Discipline and self-control suppressed his rage in the past but in his forties, Rydon's patience was wearing thinner than the silver streaks of his beard.

Lifting herself to her feet with the support of her husband's broad shoulders, Gabriella placed both hands on his frosty cheeks to kiss him goodbye. "Honey, I'm tired. I'm thinking hot chocolate and a nap. I'll keep yours warm."

"Please do," he smiled, waving as he slid downhill.

Rydon had everything he ever wanted as a child; a beautiful home decorated with fancy cars. He was wealthy and married to his soulmate, whom he loved wholeheartedly. Even still, something was missing.

Declining hundreds of feet in a matter of seconds, Rydon was finally at peace with his thoughts, days removed from closing his last case. Gliding, left, right, up, over, and higher, Rydon was effectively able to relieve stress with every leap and bound down Haji Hill.

Sliding to a stop, he grabbed hold to the tow rope, engineered by his great, great grandfather. On his way to the top, Rydon was immediately able to pinpoint the source to his disdain. He had grown up too quickly.

Everything he worked on had to be just right, even in grade school. He was a junior in high school, when he saw his first B on an assignment.

In the same time span, he helped rewrite the record books during his high school's first track and field state finals appearance. All before adding college champion to his resume.

As a senior at California Midwest University, he ended his collegiate career as valedictorian, graduating summa cum laude. Rydon was an old soul, a light year ahead of himself and it finally caught up to him.

Looking down on the state of Michigan from afar, he thought of all the things he missed out on because of how hard he worked. Arriving at the peak of Haji Hill, he knocked the snow from his boots and entered the family log cabin. Awaiting him with a look of concern, Gabriella stood ghostly, holding a cup of hot chocolate.

"You okay?" Rydon asked her.

"I think you should take this and have a seat," she answered, handing him a steaming cup of hot chocolate.

As her eyes burst into tears, Rydon's heart sank to the floor like a sack of silver. Never had he seen his wife so distraught. Holding her head against his chest, he waited for her to tell him what was going on…

Prize Fighter

Preview

```
Highland Park, Michigan
15900 Woodward Avenue
5:55am Eastern Standard Time
1959 January 5, Monday
```

"You run like a cop. You've been undercover so long, you lost your swagger. Loosen up Champ!" Marcel taunted, chucking an apple at Rydon.

"I run like a cop? That's a good thing Marcel. Try finding one woman who says I don't look like the chosen one when I run and my badge flies through the wind," Rydon darted back, jogging next to Jo's pickup truck.

Marcel sat in the flatbed, throwing rotten fruit at Rydon, that he dodged or punched. Tosses came at various speeds, up and down Woodward Avenue.

"Champions don't have to run to impress the ladies. We just hold the belt and pose for the camera. The Chosen One, you were chosen... I like it. That's your new nickname Champ," Marcel yelled, throwing a melon at Rydon's torso.

Marcel was the livewire of the crew. He and Rydon brought out the best in each other. During their training days at The Bag as amateur boxers, they were both top ten juniors in their weight classes.

The Bag was a historic Highland Park recreation center. Established in 1815 by four men: Toussaint Freeman, Wallace Goodson, Roy Shabazz and Eli Tyme. The Bag groomed some of the greatest boxers in the history of the sport.

Flash Shabazz, Icy Isa, Raphael Ruh, Bernard "Bees" Beason, and The Masterful Marcel Riaz represented generations of champions who trained at The Bag. Boxers signed contracts as prize fighters that expired well beyond their days inside the four corners.

After retirement, prize fighters turned into recruiters. Searching for the next big thing to fill their void. Rydon turned down the Professional Boxing Association once in the past. Instead, he accepted a track and field scholarship at California Midwest University.

In the meantime, four of Rydon's Life or Liberty brothers went on to become light, middle, and heavyweight champions of the world. "Alright Champ, hit the bag for ten minutes then jump rope for ten minutes.

Lift five sets of ten. We're working with one hundred twenty five pounds this week. We have to train your muscles first. Light work. After that, put another ten minutes on the speed bag alternating hands and that's it for today."

"Good day, not so old man. You're in better shape than I thought," Marcel boasted loudly, clapping his hands.

"I'm a Detective Marcel, we're always in shape," Rydon shrugged.

"We'll see. Let's go upstairs and talk about the contract."

Walking up the wooden structure of the two story building, Rydon admired pictures, Championship Belts, Iron Fist Awards, newspaper clippings, ticket stubs, boxing trunks, gloves, shoes, mouthpieces, and tons of other memorabilia.

Rydon hadn't been back to the gym since he left for college at an early age. The familiar faces lining the walls enlightened him on what he missed in his absence. Lost in a trance inside a timeless capsule, Marcel brought him back to reality from the upstairs office.

"You'll make it up there with us," Marcel called out.

"Baby steps Marcel, one day at a time," Rydon said, shadowboxing up the stairs.

"Good attitude! Hard work pays well. This is the contract we're offering you. It's a two year deal.

The second year is what we call *The Boxer's Option*. Look it over and let me know what you think. I know you're a married man now so, go over it with the Mrs. and get it back to me by Friday, signed or not because its postdated on our end."

"I'm a grown man Marcel. I can make decisions without my wife," Rydon, responded, skimming the pages.

"Even better!" Marcel clapped, pumping his fists. Read it over. Let me know if you have any questions. If not, we can get your licensing process started now."

Professional Boxing Association: Boxer's Option Premium

The Bag has been approved by the Professional Boxing Association's Board of Trustees and is thereby granted full authority to represent our brand. The Bag is authorized to offer employment to qualified amateur boxers on behalf of the Professional Boxing Association.

Section 1
Healthcare Act:
    a. The Professional Boxing Association offers lifetime health care benefits to all boxers signed with the company.

Retirement Fund:
    a. The Professional Boxing Association requires at least 5% of all earnings from professional bouts, to be paid into the boxer's Retirement Fund.

    b. Retirement Funds can be disbursed in the follow ways:
        1. One large lump sum.
        2. Monthly, weekly, or biweekly increments until funds have fully disbursed.
        3. Endorsed to another.

    c. All retired boxers are paid annual stipends worth 1% of their total career earnings.

    d. 2 tickets are reserved for all retired boxers wishing to attend Professional Boxing Association events. Reservations begin 24 hours before public sale and are subject to availability afterwards.

    e. 2 tickets to the annual Boxer's Ball.

Section 2:
Terms of Agreement:
    a. One season as defined by the Professional Boxing Association is equivalent to 10 fights during a 30 month span.

    b. *Boxer's Option* guarantees the boxer up to 10 additional fights. So long as it lasts no longer than 30 months.

    c. Any and all contract negotiations must be completed during the Professional Boxing Association off season (July, August, and September).

    d. All boxers are required to join the Boxer's Union.

Section 3:
Personal Conduct:
    a. All boxers must entertain the media during press conferences at least once before and after (same day) prize fights.

b. Press conferences shall not last longer than 30 minutes unless the boxer consents.
c. Boxers are expected to act as law abiding citizens. Misconduct will be handled on a case by case basis.

Section 4:

Compensation:

All purses are split 70/30. The event sponsor receives 70%.

I, <u>Rydon Tyme,</u> accept the terms of agreement as a prize fighter of the Professional Boxing Association.

X _____
Professional Boxer

x The Bag Recreation Center 1-9-1959
Witness

"You know what? I want Gabby to be with me when I sign it. I'll get it back to you by Friday," Rydon countered, scratching his head.

"Same ole Don," Marcel laughed. "It's going to be good having everyone back in the gym again."

"Who's everyone?" Rydon wondered, with peaked curiosity.

"Flash, Ruh, and Bees for sure. They're your sparring partners."

"Sparring partners? I haven't boxed live since I was thirteen. They're Champions. I need to warm up first. That's like walking with an antelope in the safari," Rydon warned.

"We have time, but we don't have time to waste. Warm up fights would be useless for a person with your skill set," Marcel reminded him.

"I'll spar with the champs after sparing with your best boxers in the gym for a few days. I grew up sparring with Flash, Ruh, and Bees. I want to see what the young bucks are made of," Rydon reasoned.

"I'll tell you what, Ty Farmer is the real deal. He just needs some time," Marcel said, walking towards the window.

"How old is he?"

"Just turned twenty-one in November. He's got power. Fists are big as bricks and his hand eye coordination is impeccable. If he lands a haymaker, you might retire a little early," Marcel informed him, watching his fighters train from the office window. "But, he's raw with two left feet and bad defense."

"If he has bad feet, I'd hit him twice before he throws a punch. Not to mention, landing a punch would mean I didn't see his punches coming. My eyes have gotten stronger over the years," Rydon gloated.

"Finally, you understand. Sparring with anyone besides polished boxers is a waste of time. On the other hand, Farmer could learn a lot sparring with someone new. Speaking of which, this kid from Louisville stopped by yesterday. Said he's here for a week and wanted to know if he could train here.

I don't mind loaning the gym to a traveler for a few days if he's serious about the craft, so I put him to the test. He beat my top three boxers in twenty-seven minutes real time.

Sixteen years old. He reminded me a lot of you but better. His trash talk was smoother than yours too. It was like poetry. That kid is going to be special. I told him to sign and date the gloves he used. They're hanging up over there," Marcel pointed to the wall. "He wrote, *I am the greatest boxer of all times, already!* The kid knows he's bad," Marcel laughed.

"I hope he is better than me. I want to meet him. Did he whoop Farmer too?" Rydon wondered, gauging Farmer's skill set.

"I didn't let him fight Farmer. That could've gotten ugly, either way. I'll let you spar with the gym members over the weekend. After that, I'm throwing you to the wolves," Marcel said, breaking down the game plan.

"I wouldn't have it any other way. I just need to tune up first," Rydon said, shadowboxing defensively.

"Any other concerns give me a call. The contract offer expires Friday, ninety-six hours is standard PBA protocol. They run a tight ship. Unfortunately, you can't box live without a contract so get ready for a lot of cardio and weight training. See you tomorrow at five minutes to six."

"Good deal, peace," Rydon agreed in principle on his way out the door.

L.O.T.T.

Leaders Of Tomorrow, Today...

Michigan International University (2015) Wake Up Little Lion (2016) Royal Comics... Coming Soon

ABOUT THE AUTHOR

Ali Muhammad was born and raised in Highland Park, Michigan. After graduating from Western Michigan University with a Bachelor of Science degree in Professional Education, Muhammad began his Teaching career in one of West Michigan's Title I public schools.

In 2015, Muhammad pursued a second career in writing and has three published works to date. Debut novel, Michigan International University. Children's book, Wake Up Little Lion, and short story, Nobody Cares.

During production for LOTT Magazine (2018), Muhammad was promoted from Lead Writer to Editor-In-Chief. Nobody Cares is the fourth installment of a five project production deal Muhammad signed with Leaders of Tomorrow, Today LLC.

www.ingramcontent.com/pod-product-compliance
Lightning Source LLC
Chambersburg PA
CBHW071330130626
46556CB00004B/1840